THE BIGOT

BY JAMES BARCLAY

SEANACHAIDH PUBLISHING LTD

SEANACHAIDH PUBLISHING LTD
Greenock, Scotland PA15 1BT
1989

Graphic Design by: William Stewart D.A.

Typeset by On-Line Text Ltd., Glasgow.
Printed by: Holmes MacDougall, Glasgow

ISBN: 0 948963 50 6

CONTENTS

CHAPTER ONE

SATURDAY MORNING

Andra Thomson snored the deep snore that whisky brings. Vesuvius had come to 'Brigton'. The low, droning, gutteral sound reverberated around the small bedroom and vanished through any aperture it could find. When Andra Thomson snored the whole tenement in Glasgow knew about it.

Next door, in the kitchen, his long-suffering wife, Annie, was already preparing breakfast. She walked over, closed the bedroom door in a vain effort to dampen the noise, took a quick glance at a picture of King Billy that hung on the kitchen wall and muttered — "bet your hoarse disnae make as much racket as yer devoted servant in there." Annie was not a devotee of King Billy and merely tolerated his presence in her kitchen for the sake of keeping harmony as best she could. Next to Billy's colourful portrait was one of Andra himself in the prized regalia of Rangers football supporters.

Andra's trip to oblivion was nothing unusual for a Saturday morning but Annie thought that he might have wakened up a bit earlier this particular morning. For this was not a normal Saturday.

Saturday in every city, every town and hamlet is always a special day, but in Glasgow perhaps a bit more so. When old-time Glasgow comic, Will Fyffe, sang about the city belonging to him on a Saturday night, he meant every Glaswegian. For most of its citizens it was the day when the dungarees were discarded for the weekend. The grime and grease of the week's work was scrubbed off and the crisply ironed shirts were pulled over razor-smoothed faces splashed liberally with stinging after-shave lotion. The pubs and dance halls were Dettol fresh and ready for the invasion. Work was forgotten.

For Andra Thomson work had been forgotten for many years due to his "bad back" which Annie suspected was more imaginary than real. It never stopped her "sleeping beauty" from tackling the three-storey tenement stairs, where they lived on the first floor, and walking briskly towards McDougall's pub, down the street and around the corner. Not that he ever walked briskly back again from his favourite hostelry.

His built-in gyro compass set his swaying stagger on its course and he usually arrived home without mishap. Other times, when his

5

compass and legs were not synchronised, his cronies carried him, before heading back to McDougall's and rejoining the swilling. Annie often wondered WHO carried THEM home.

If Annie's spick and span four apartment home had an annex, it was McDougall's. Her wandering, better half spent many happy hours there with his pals. But, the practical "wee wumman" that she was, counted her blessings. Their two children were grown up now. Jean was twenty and doing well at Teachers' Training College and Peter, who was eighteen, studied hard and kept out of trouble. Annie was proud of her family and, despite Andra's shortcomings, she had a deep love and affection for him.

"He's no' a' that bad," she would say. "Jist easily led."

Compared to Andra, Annie was tiny . . . barely reaching her husband's shoulders. But her dainty feet could come down hard when it was necessary and Andra would invariably depart into the bedroom in a boyish sulk. There were times when it didn't do to argue with Annie.

It was in the bedroom that Andra found all his consolation. It was there that he could glory in his collection of pictures of Glasgow Rangers Football Club. At one time there had been thirty-four photographs of his heroes papering the boudoir walls, but Annie's size two's had come down firmly and Andra now had only two pictures pinned up on the wall at the end of the bed, where he could see them the minute he awoke. It was the first time that Rangers had been relegated, he told Annie. His huge collection was now stored in a box underneath the bed and this would be retrieved and pored over with rapture in times of distress.

These were HIS boys . . . HIS team. NEVER in the field of football conflict had so much been owed by so many to so few. If Andra had a third home it was Ibrox Park, the home of Glasgow Rangers. To Andra Thomson the ground there was as sacred as the Domaine of Lourdes is to Catholics. The grass was greener, this hallowed turf!

Once he had been caught by a burly policeman trying to dig up two square feet of it for a window box he was planning. He was sent packing muttering that the big cop should really be in the Swiss Guard.

Enquiries about getting buried in the centre of Ibrox Park after his demise were contemptuously rebuffed by the Rangers Board. Piqued, he threatened to withdraw his support of the team and approach arch-rivals, Celtic Football Club, with a view to be planted there . . . "Even

6

if it's under the hoat-pie stall", he snarled. Not that he would ever have considered approaching Paradise — the tag given to Celtic's London Road home ground. God forbid!

Celtic supporters were CATHOLICS. Andra shuddered at the mention of that leperous word. The fact that Annie was a catholic didn't come into it. He tried never to think of that stigma in his marriage and, so far, had managed to keep the terrible secret from his cronies down at McDougall's.

He would never want to lose Annie for he, too, had a deep affection for his wife. And he had to admit there were no holy pictures gracing the walls of his house . . . except King Billy, of course. Annie was a clever woman.

Andra hadn't given up hope of being buried at Ibrox Park just as he hadn't given up his other great wishes . . . to join the Orange Lodge and the Freemasons.

He had approached those august bodies many times offering his everlasting allegiance. But he was politely "bombed out." Both institutions had questioned his motives and were not satisfied that Andra was the right material for their ranks.

You just don't tell the Orange Order that you wish to join them because "Ah'm keen tae learn the flute." And, being presented to a Masonic official, it is not advisable to twist the man's arm up his back . . . pretending you have been doing your homework and are acquainted with some of their secret signals. Andra was undeterred. He would try again. His motto was — "Never gie up," except maybe work.

Annie would commiserate with him although secretly she was delighted that he was "bombed oot." His fanatical obsession with Rangers was enough to cope with . . . more than plenty.

Now it was Saturday again . . . the BIG Saturday. The "Auld Firm" would meet at Hampden Park and battle it out for the coveted League Trophy.

The "Auld Firm" . . . an affectionate title given to Celtic and Rangers when they met on the field. But this was the Clash of the Titans. There was little affection between sections of the fans. This was a battle between Catholics and Protestants — The River Boyne — re-lived. The ugly face of the game that all true football fans of both teams condemned without mercy — the minority they found they had to live with.

7

Andra would stand on the terracing and yell and curse with the best of them. He knew all of the words. You learn them as you grow amongst the grey tenements. Politeness is weakness and you soon learn that a curt curse word can diffuse a potentially dangerous situation. Andra cursed the fact that he was brought up in Bridgeton, in Glasgow's East End and in the shadow of Celtic Park. Fate had delivered a mocking blow there. Still, there was always the consolation of McDougall's where he and his ilk would meet and relish in the conversation of their heroes.

"We arra people", was the cry and Andra meant it. He had been celebrating last night in anticipation of the battle of Hampden. It would be massacre, he reckoned, with Rangers the boys-in-blue marching off with the cup. At least 10 - Nil would be the final score. He was sure of that.

Some of his cronies thought 2-1 might be a more realistic score — but what did they know? No, it was complete annihilation of Celtic. Nothing else would suffice. Tomorrow, after the game and the cup presentation ceremony, they would flock merrily on to McDougall's and toast the boys in traditional style. Andra had staggered home from the hostelry on the eve of the big game singing his party tunes with gusto. Some of the less sympathetic neighbours slammed their windows and more than a few derogatory comments were yelled from the safety of darkened closemouths. Andra heard none of this. The expectation of what was to come filled his whole being. He floated home in bliss.

Annie had heard her singing husband as he turned into the street. A slight drizzle had begun and Annie emerged from the cupboard with a clean towel, ready to dry her husband's head and pour him into bed. Andra wouldn't stay awake long after he arrived into the heat of the house, despite his euphoria. Annie knew this. She was ready, towel in hand as Andra staggered through the door.

"Hiv ye been waitin' up for me, hen?" he slurred.

"C'mon, inta bed wi' ye", Annie said, shuffling him towards the bedroom while rubbing the towel into his head at the same time.

Annie had pulled his damp clothes from her swaying, incoherent husband and tucked him safely into bed. With one defiant chant of, "We arra people", Andra Thomson slipped quickly into oblivion. Perhaps the morrow would bring its roses . . . but roses have thorns.

Annie fussed around the cooker. The snores from the bedroom were lighter now. "Andra", she bawled, "yer breakfast's ready . . . get up."

8

There was no response. "Andra", she repeated, "wull ye get up . . . this'll be ruined."

There was a grunt from the bedroom. Andra Thomson rubbed bleary eyes and tried to get his bearings. It had been a great night in McDougall's. Annie's voice stabbed at his throbbing head. "Ah'm no' gonny shout again", she yelled.

Andra just wanted to curl up and get back into the limbo he had just left. Who was thinking about breakfast? His head flopped back on to the pillow and the room spun. Rangers ace striker Derek Johnstone's picture stared back at Andra. He seemed to be doing a jig. Andra tried hard to focus on the beloved portrait.

"ANDRA" . . . the voice had all the volume of a cannon in an echo chamber. Andra quickly clapped hands over his ears.

"Ye'll be late for the match," Annie hollered. The match! How could he forget that? Elation swept over him. Never had he felt like this before — except maybe the time he won the bottle in McDougall's Christmas raffle.

"Whit time is it?" he asked, entering the kitchen, still stretching and scratching and still garbed in his long-johns. He rubbed his eyes and peered at the clock on the mantleshelf.

"Ach, it's only eleven o'clock," he grumbled.

"It's time ye were up," Annie snapped, placing his breakfast on top of the table.

Andra flopped into the dining chair and viewed the food before him. "Whit's this bloody muck? "he growled.

"It's a' we can afford," Annie said, unconcerned as she continued at the cooker.

"Bloody black puddin'," Andra grimaced, pushing the plate away from him. "Know whit they call that in the army?" he complained.

"Never you mind whit they call it." Annie retorted. "Ye can take it or leave it. Ye canny drink yer dole an' live like Reo Stakis," she said, referring to the millionaire restaurateur.

Andra's eyebrows shot up.

"Ah live mair like Rio Bravo — if it's no' black puddin', its baked beans," he moaned. "Beans might mean Heinz tae you, they mean bloody wind tae me," he added.

"Ach, ye're full o' wind anyway — don't blame the beans," Annie snapped back.

Andra toyed with the black pudding and turning, pointed his finger

9

at Annie, "Dae you know whit black puddin's made of, eh?" Annie ignored him.

"BLOOD — bloody blood," Andra said contemptuously . . . "They get the blood fae the coos an' sheep and God knows where else an' they mix it a' up an' call it black puddin' . . . THAT'S whit YOU are gien ME for ma breakfast."

"It's good for ye," Annie replied, not looking round.

"D'ye think ah'm bloody Dracula? Whit aboot a dod o' ham?"

"Ye're full o' ham," Annie snapped, "And unless ye get oaf yer bahooky and find a joab, it'll be black puddin' and beans for you . . . like it or lump it."

Andra ignored his wife's remarks and, rising with a grunt, began searching the mantleshelf for his cigarettes.

"Where's the fags? "he asked sulkily.

"You're the only wan that smokes — the only wan that can afford them," Annie retorted.

The cigarettes were nowhere to be found and Andra turned his search to the ash-trays dotted around the kitchen. He let out a yell of success when he discovered a fair-sized butt and quickly lit up.

"Has the paper come?" he inquired. "It's oan yer chair." Andra flopped on the chair and began to read his morning paper — ignoring the page-one headlines and turning immediately to the back-page sports columns.

"D'ye no' think ye should go in there an' get yer claethes oan?" Annie asked with disgust in her voice: "Hive ye nae shame?"

"Ah'm in ma ain hoose, int ah?" Andra replied without looking up from his paper.

"That disnae mean ye've tae walk aboot like John L Sullivan."

"Who's tae see me?"

"Yer son an' yer daughter, that's who," Annie said angrily.

"Ach they don't count."

"Don't count!" Annie said, raising her voice, "Jean's a young wumman noo, ye know. They're no' weans."

Andra knew that Annie was right but he could not give in immediately. He daren't show weakness. Snapping the centre pages of his newspaper open, he snuggled more comfortably into the easy chair and continued to read.

"A faither should want his weans tae be proud o' him," Annie said quietly.

Andra closed the paper. For a moment a feeling of guilt came over him.

"Well, er . . .," he stumbled on the words, "er . . . wance ah get accepted intae the Ludge things'll be different. Ah'll maybe get mair respect around here."

Annie let out a loud exclamation. "YOU . . . get into the Ludge! If you get in, every Freemason in Glesga will join the Knights o' St. Columba."

"Ach you're bigoted," Andra snapped.

" There's nae answer tae that," Annie said. "Mind ye if by some miracle ye DID get in, ye might get a joab." Andra grimaced at the word.

"Ye know ah canny work . . . it's ma back."

"There'll be nuthin' wrang wi' yer back this afternoon," Annie snapped.

"That's different," Andra said, smugly, "Ye're no' doin' manual labour. Ye're just staunin' there watchin' the boys." The thought sent a rapturous quiver through his body.

"Aye, well the boys don't pey the rent," Annie answered. "They're a' right . . . makin' money oot o' mugs like you. Ah'll bet that THEY'RE no' sittin' doon tae black puddin' for their breakfast." Andra was taken aback at this statement.

"An' that's they wey it SHOULD be", he said, more in hurt than anger. "THEY ur ARTISTS." Annie decided to let that go and, turning towards the door leading to the bedrooms called out . . . "Jean . . . Peter . . . breakfast." Then, swinging round on her husband, ordered "An' you . . . away an' get dressed."

Andra arose slowly and shuffled towards the bedroom mumbling — "Always fussin'."

Jean, already dressed and sparkling, was first to enter and take her place at the table. "Morning mum," she smiled.

"Mornin', Jean," Annie smiled. She was proud of "her Jean."

"I suppose dad'll be going to the Cup Final today?" Annie threw her arms up. "He's done nuthin' but talk aboot it a' week. He took the Hoover ower his rosette yesterday."

" It's a religion with him, isn't it, " Jean said with a grin.

11

"A religion? If he was a Catholic he'd be a bishop," Annie said.

"What makes him so bigoted, mum? I mean YOU'RE a Catholic," Jean said, tucking into her breakfast.

Annie smiled. "Ah, but he didnae know that when we met that night at Barraland. An' when he DID find oot it was too late. But he wisnae as bad then as he is noo. As he got aulder he seemed tae get worse."

"He never objected to you going to Mass on a Sunday," Jean said.

"Huh," Annie snorted, "Just let him try. He knows that if he did ah'd tell his cronies that their true-blue Andra . . . the same big-mouth that curses the Pope — was married tae a Catholic. He could never live with that shame." Annie smiled wryly. "He can call it blackmail if he likes." Jean smiled. "And that's why you travel to Saint Alphonsus' chapel, in Calton, instead of the local Sacred Heart chapel?"

"We've got an understandin'," Annie said.

Peter entered the room rubbing his hands and smiling. "Ah, Saturday again . . . lovely," he said. Annie placed his breakfast on the table and Peter joined Jean.

"I saw you last night in Sauchiehall Street," he said between mouthfuls of blackpudding and sausage Annie had kept aside for "the weans."

"You should have said hello," Jean said.

"Ach, you were too quick," Peter said. "You went into an MG and away before I could shout."

"That was Clarence's new car," Jean said proudly, "he's . . ."

Andra had entered the room. He was already togged up for the game with his blue and white scarf around his neck, the large rosette in his lapel and the huge, wooden, rickety in his hand. He gave it a twirl — "We Arra People," he cried with gusto. He admired himself in the mirror above the fireplace.

"You're a bit early for that, are ye not?" Peter asked.

"Jist practisin', son, jist practisin'. Get the tonsils tuned up. We'll massacre them the day. It's aboot time you were in there wi' me, Peter, supportin' the boys." Andra felt that his son should take more interest in the finer things of life.

"It's aboot time you were supportin' yer faimly," Annie commented.

"Quiet, wumman," Andra snapped. "No' fancy gaun tae the match Peter?" he asked.

"You know I'm no' interested in fitba'." Peter replied.

Andra was dismayed. "No' interested in fitba'? Every man is interested in

12

fitba' . . . every man." Andra tried to stifle his annoyance.

"Only mugs," Peter said.

Annie and Jean saw Andra's face turn from a pale pink to deep purple.

"MUGS?" he exploded, "MUGS . . .? YOU don't understaun', dae ye? When we take the field the day it's the Boyne a' ower again. That ba' is a cannon ba'. It's ammunition . . . 'cos WE ARRA PEOPLE." Andra bellowed.

"The Boyne was hundreds of years ago," Peter shrugged, "It's past . . . forgotten."

"FORGOTTEN? . . . It'll NEVER be forgotten — NEVER," what kind of boy is this, Andra wondered, that he could forget his heritage?

Peter was not going to be intimidated. "Look," he said, "how can you go out there on that terracin' and kick the Pope? What's the Pope got to do wi' it? He probably supports Inter-Milan . . ."

"He wull undoubtedly support the Celtic. He wears a lotta green," Andra was adamant."

"Ye don't know what ye're talking aboot," Peter replied. Annie stepped in immediately before the confrontation got out of hand.

"Stoap yer bickerin' the pair of ye," she intervened. "Ah'm goin' doon tae the shoaps. There might be a sale oan at the Co-operative butchers. Ah'll no' be long."

Annie lifted her coat from the hook on the door and adjusted her headsquare. Turning, she ordered — "Nae fightin'."

Jean arose and began to clear the table. "Will you be back in time to meet Clarence?" she asked. Annie assured her that she would. Andra's eyebrows shot up. This was a name that had never been mentioned before. The only Clarence he knew of was a cross-eyed lion at Calderpark Zoo.

"Who the hell's Clarence?" he asked

"Oh, mum," Jean said to Annie, it was an appeal for support.

"Jist you never mind aboot Clarence," Annie snapped. "Ye'll know soon enough. Aye, ah'll be back in plenty o' time, Jean. Ah'll get somethin' nice for a wee cuppa tea." Then with a "you dare" glance at Andra she hurried out.

There was a long pause. Peter had said nothing and cleared his own dishes, placing them on the sink.

"Well," Andra demanded, "who is this bloody Clarence, then?"

Jean gave Peter a knowing look and, turning to her father, said, "I wanted to ask you something, dad."

13

Peter took the hint. "Well, he said, "if you two want to talk, I'll make mysel' scarce." He turned towards the door.

"Where are YOU goin'?" Andra was curious as to what was afoot.

"The library," Peter replied, retrieving his jacket from the communal door hook. "I've a lot of swottin' to do for ma exams." Exams? This was the first Andra had heard of any exams.

"Whit exams?" he inquired curiously. "Och, just exams," Peter replied, giving no hint. "Are you tryin' tae get above yer station, or somethin'?" Andra sneered.

"Is there anything wrong in tryin' to better yerself?" Peter asked slipping into his jacket.

"BETTER YERSEL'?" Andra turned to Jean. "Listen, ye are what ye are and ah'm whit Ah am. That's the way things are."
Ah am. That's the way things are."

"But they don't HAVE to be that way," Peter retorted. You should use the talents that God gave ye."

"GOD?" Andra bellowed in disbelief, "don't tell me ye believe in a' that rubbish?"

"Ye don't think this universe o' ours is one big accident?" Peter said.

"You're wan big accident, boy," Andra said, shaking his head in despair.

Peter ignored the disparaging remark. "Look," he said, "The Earth, the Sun, the planets . . . everything has perfect order. Ye don't think that was an ACCIDENT, do ye . . . that it all just happened?"

"You think God did that?"

"Of course," Peter said. "In the beginning there was nothing."

"Well, as faur as AH'M concerned there's still bloody nuthin'," Andra argued.

"Ye only take out o' the world what ye put into it," Peter answered.

Andra wasn't going to let that STATEMENT pass unanswered.

"Nut true," he said quickly, "in ma . . . er . . . healthier days ah put in a lotta back-breakin' work. An' when ah leave this world ah'll be takin' a bloody slipped disc wi' me. Wis THAT God's plan, wis it.? Away doon there, Andra an' work like a navvy an' when ah see ye up here again ah want ye tae be crippled."

"Some people must suffer for others," Peter replied.

"Well, AH'M sufferin' for the whole bloody Dalmarnock Road,"

14

Andra snapped back. "Anywey, whit's he pickin' oan me for? Ah don't even believe in him. If he wants tae dish out sore backs he should pick oan his ain."

Peter made a hasty departure mutterring: "Ach, there's no point arguing wi' you."

Andra turned to Jean. "Got his priorities a' mixed up, that boy. Imagine . . . goin' tae the library an Rangers playin' Celtic . . . whit kinda boy is that?"

Jean was not going to get involved in a family squabble. She ignored her dad's comments. Besides she had other things on her mind. Putting the last dried plate on a rack, she turned to Andra.

"Dad," she said a little anxiously.

Andra turned. "Whit is it? Somethin' up? Somebody comin' the micky wi' ye eh? Ye know ah'll never staun for that."

Jean bit her lip. "Ah want you to do me a favour."

Andra felt suddenly paternal. "Anythin', ma wee Jean, you know that."

Jean hesitated. "Well, . . . er . . . it's about Clarence." Clarence? There was that name again. "Clarence," Andra threw his arms in the air, "who the hell is Clarence?"

"That's what I'm tryin' to tell you. We . . . we're gettin' engaged."

Andra stood and stared blankly. He was stunned. Here was his "golden wee lassie" telling him that she was about to be betrothed to somebody he had never even heard of.

There must be a reason for this sudden terrible, drastic and positively unacceptable news, Andra felt the anger swell up inside him. The volcano blew.

"The swine," he exploded. "Ah don't even know him. Ye're in the club, aren't ye, eh?"

Jean tried to protest but Andra, purple-faced, paid no attention.

"The dirty, rotten swine. Wi' a name like Clarence ye widnae think he had it in him. That's whit fooled ye, wisn't it, eh?"

"No dad," Jean protested. "You've got it all wrong. He's a gentleman . . . a student at the college."

A student? Andra had no time for students.

"A student, eh? Ah'll bet he's oan the marajooana . . . no tae mention the wine . . . the Lanny." Andra reckoned he knew all about students.

15

"Oh, you're just biased, dad. Not everybody's the same."

Andra was hurt by the the remark. "Biased? ME biased . . . there's naebody less biaseder than me, hen." How could Jean imagine such a thing?

There was a moments silence then Jean said quietly: "Clarence would like to meet you."

Andra found his voice once again: "Ah should bloody well think so," he snapped, "How come ah hiv never had the pleasure of meetin' this rapist, eh?"

Jean was quickly losing patience with her dad. "Oh you're impossible", she said angrily, then, calmly, "look, he's a nice boy. His parents are well-to-do. His father's a doctor. They live in Newton Mearns."

Andra's brows went up. Newton Mearns to Andra was the Beverly Hills of Glasgow. Where folk had bathrooms and many even had telephones in their homes. Anyone from Newton Mearns was probably high up in the Masonic Order. But suddenly his brows knitted. There was something not right here.

"How come this seducer goes for a lassie fae Brigton, eh? Tell me that. It's no how the social structure works."

"Oh dad, you're living in the past," Jean said with anxiety. "It doesn't matter to Clarence where I come from . . . Bridgeton is Bridgeton."

"Aw naw it's no'," Andra blurted out. "Frae Brigton Croass on ye don't know where the hell ye are. D'ye know somethin', ah arranged tae meet Bowly McGeachie in a wee coarner pub in Marquis Street wan night last week. But see when ah got there . . ."

Jean looked up impatiently: "The pub was away," she sighed.

"The bloody STREET was away," Andra snapped. "Brigton is oor last stronghold an' they are oot tae flatten it. Ye jist hiv tae look at the wallahs in the city chambers . . . full o' Papes. The thing is that we are too near Parkhead. That's the reason they are devastatin' it . . . scatterin' US. 'Cos without unity ye hiv nae strength. The City Fathers . . . even their bloody title gies them away . . . hiv a loat tae answer for."

"Oh, nonsense," Jean answered.

"Ye think so? Naw, naw. They're up tae a' the tricks. Ye read aboot them travellin' abroad tae Arabia an' a' these places. YOU think it's tae invite these blokes tae come an' actually LIVE here. Ye've got

16

Indians an' Pakis an' Chinese an' the Arabs are comin' next, mark ma words. Ah'm tellin' ye that before long it'll be the number sixty-two camel ye'll be takin' tae yer work."

Jean shook her head despairingly. "Och, you're going too far," she said.

Andra ignored the comment. "They hivnae dared tamper wi' the holy ground of Ibrox ... but they'll need watchin'," he said knowingly.

Jean could not allow her father to get away with his bigoted comments against the Glasgow Corporation. She thought of the slums people were living in. With the lavatories outside on stairheads ... there to serve three families, where a decent bath meant dragging the old zinc tub from underneath the bed and sitting it in front of the coal fire ... hoping that none of the family came home early and that some privacy would be afforded.

Glasgow was being surgically changed with parts being removed and replaced. High flats with all amenities were springing up ... towers of ivory to some and Babel to others. Her dad was one of the "Others".

Jean came to the defence of the "City Fathers." "They are trying hard to make people more comfortable in their lives," she said meaningly. "There's little space in the city and houses must come down to make way for NEW homes. They have to build upwards."

"Aye, but they're killin' the character of the place ... as well as breakin' up OOR staunch stronghold," Andra said with authority.

Nostalgia swept over him. "Ach," he reminisced "it used tae be that everybody nicked in an' out o' everybody elses hoose. Ye were wan big happy family up the close. The wimmen used tae hing oot the windae, bletherin' tae their cronies in the street. These multi-storeys hiv killed a' that. Hing oot the windae noo an' ye need a bloody megaphone an' a pair o' binoculars."

But people are more comfortable INSIDE their homes," Jean said.

"It disnae matter," Andra said, "It's sad. Prison cells, that's whit they are. In the auld days even the coalman wis wan o' the family. Nane o' yer central heatin' then. If ye were cauld an' couldnae afford a bag o' coal ye just broke up a chair an' stuck it in the fire. We were lucky, we had a Morris chair ... five o' us slept in it. We WURNAE cauld, ah can tell ye that. But, see in wee Bowly McGeachie's hoose ... they were really poor." Andra shook his head, sadly.

He went on: "When ye went in there they were a' sittin' on the flair

17

like Indians. It was a shame. That's how Bowly became bloody bowly legged . . . sittin' there wi' his knees up tae his chin."

"Rickets," Jean said.

"Naw, they couldnae afford them," Andra said, shaking his head.

"I said RICKETS."

"Oh, ah thought ye said briquetts," Andra said. Jean pushed her point. "Bowly McGeachie probably got his bow legs because of rickets. It was to do with the poor diet."

"Well it disnae matter HOW he got them, he bloody well got them. Ah'll tell ye this, ye'll never get ME steyin' in wan o' they fire traps. Yer mither thinks differently. She keeps hintin'. But ah'm tellin' ye . . . by the time they're ready tae pull this buildin' doon, ah'll be kickin' up the daisies."

"Oh, you have a lot of life left in you yet" Jean said, then changing the conversation and, steering it towards the issue in hand, added: "Come on now stop living in the past. Clarence doesn't care where I live."

"Don't be too sure," Andra said with suspicion, and as an afterthought added: "is he a Mason by any chance."

Jean shrugged. "I don't know," she said. This Clarence from Newton Mearns might just be the link Andra was searching for. It was worth thinking about. A Mason in the family could be a great asset.

Stroking his chin he said: "Ask him if his granny's got a wart oan her bum." Jean was caught short by the suddeness of the vulgar expression. "DAD," she scolded.

"THAT," said Andra with complete knowledge, "is a secret code. Bowly McGeachie told me it in the pub. If you ask somebody that an' they answer that the wart is oan her belly . . . ye've made contact."

"I wouldn't believe ANYTHING that Bowly McGeachie said," Jean said contemptuously.

But Andra jumped to his crony's defence: "Naw, Naw," he said, "Bowly is a man o' the world. When ah went for that last joab it wis the first thing ah said tae the gaffer — "Hiz your granny got a wart on her bum'? Ah said, lookin' him straight in the eye. Ah never goat the joab right enough . . . maybe he wis a Catholic or somethin'."

"But father . . ." Jean started . . .

Andra's bellow could be heard streets away . . . "NEVER", he raged, "NEVER but NEVER call me FATHER." He mopped his brow and calm was restored after a few seconds.

"Noo, where wis ah", he continued, "Aye, another secret phrase Bowly kindly allowed me tae be cogn . . er . . cog . . know of is that ye ask a bloke if he's kissed the goat's erse. If he says he hiz then he is definitely, but definitely, been initiated. And if ye ask 'Whit age is yer granny?' — ye're really askin' — 'Whit's yer Ludge number?'

"THAT is vulgar, dad," Jean said disgustedly.

Andra shrugged, "That's how it is, hen." Jean tried once more to steer the conversation to the more important topic in hand.

"Dad, will you PLEASE listen," she pleaded, "Clarence is coming up today . . . to ask your permission."

"He canny come up the day," Andra shook his head, "this is the cup-final."

"He knows that," Jean said, softening her voice. "I was wondering if you might take him to the match with you?"

"Ye mean he's a fitba' fan?", Andra couldn't imagine anyone from Newton Mearns being a football fan.

"Well, he's never actually been to a match, but when I told him that you were going to the cup final, he thought it would be a good way to break the ice," Jean looked at her father pleadingly.

Andra knitted his eyebrows and thought deeply. "Whit team does he support?" "He doesn't support ANY team," Jean replied, "he knows nothing about football."

"Knows nuthin' aboot fitba', eh! Andra stroked his chin. "He must be a Celtic supporter."

"Clarence has other interests," Jean was quick to point out.

Andra sneered: "Like knittin' for instance? There must be SOME kinda sport he goes in for . . . besides messin' about wi' innocent young lassies?"

"He likes squash," Jean said

"Teetotal as well, eh?"

"Squash is a game demanding a lot of stamina," Jean said, jumping to her boyfriend's defence. And as an afterthought added: "He is also very good at equestrian events."

"Ah hardly call THAT a sport," Andra sneered. "Anybody can swim."

"Riding, Dad, he likes riding," Jean corrected him.

"THAT is bloody obvious," Andra snapped.

"Horses," Jean snapped.

"Oh, he likes the hoarses?" Andra thought he might find something redeemable yet in this stranger. "Well, that's somethin' in his favour. Ah'm kinda partial tae them masel."

"He doesn't gamble," Jean said, getting the record straight.

'This is not possible,' Andra thought. "He likes hoarses but he disnae gamble? There's somethin' queer there. Does he drink?"

"He likes a bottle of wine now and then,"

"A wine-o, eh?"

"He enjoys a bottle of wine with a meal," Jean said — "Blue Nun, if you want to be precise."

"Well, at least he's got the colour right," Andra agreed, "but that's aboot a'. Ah'm afraid this bloke jist disnae appeal tae me."

Jean flashed back angrily: "Well he does to me and that's what counts. You've never even met him. How can you condemn somebody you've never met?" The tears began to well up in her eyes.

"Ah've never met the Pope," Andra said. "You won't even give him a chance," Jean sobbed.

Andra tried to avoid Jean's tears. He could easily weaken and he knew it. His family was cracking up. Peter visiting the library instead of the bookie like any normal boy. And now Jean searching for a husband in Poshville.

"Whit's wrang wi' the boys roon aboot?" he asked.

"Nothing," Jean said, finding some composure, "nothing at all. But I LOVE Clarence. You just don't choose ANYBODY to fall in love with. I'm doing it my way, dad, I'm sorry." There was a finality in her voice.

"Ye'll dae whit AH tell ye," Andra snapped back.

"I won't, dad," Jean said quietly.

"You're MA daughter an' ye live under MA roof," Andra's voice rose in anger.

"Well we can soon fix that," Jean said, her own voice raising. There was a silent pause. Each of them turning away.

"Look, dad," Jean said, breaking the silence, "all I asked you to do is MEET Clarence, I've given you your place." Andra went into one of his sulks. "Ah brought ye up an' this is the thanks ah get . . . jumpin' at the first bloke that flatters ye."

"He's not the first bloke but he's right one," Jean said pleadingly.

"He sounds a right wan," Andra snorted. Jean drew closer to her father and gently stroked his hair. "Oh, dad, we've never quarrelled," she said sweetly. "Say you'll see Clarence, please. It's an ordeal for him, too, you know."

Andra's obstinacy melted reluctantly.

"A' right," he said. "Ah'll even take him tae the match . . . jist tae please YOU." Then, as an afterthought — "But ah'm no' promisin' that ah'll like him."

Jean kissed her father lightly on the cheek: "That's fair enough," she said. "He'll be here in a little while."

Andra flushed slightly with embarrassment. Showing emotions of the loving kind was not the norm in the Thomson household. He found himself stammering: "Aye, well . . . er . . . well, as long as he's got the price o' his ain ticket." Then, thoughtfully: "His faither's a doactor, ye say?" Jean knew her father's train of thought.

"Yes, he has his own practise."

"Maybe he'll hiv a look at ma back," he said.

A sharp knock at the door ended the scene. Jean walked across the room saying: "I'll get it."

Andra was glad of the interruption. He could hear voices coming from the stairhead landing and Jean entered followed by Hughie Broon.

"It's Hughie, dad," she announced. Andra's eyes widened. It was always good to see Hughie. It was even better to see the "cairry-oot" Hughie gripped tightly. The bottles clinked merrily.

Hughie Broon was Andra's closest friend — a loyal disciple who had Andra on a pedestal. They were related through drink and anything Andra uttered was gospel as far as Hughie was concerned. When Andra was broke didn't he always approach Hughie first for "a bung" before trying elsewhere?

"Ye'll get yer reward in that great Ibrox Social Club in the sky," Andra would say. This would be the only place Hughie could ever hope to retrieve it. Yes Andra was a true friend. He even allowed his "wee pal" the use of his blue and white tile hat when the occasion arose. This was an honour, indeed. It was a miracle, too, that Hughie ever doffed his bunnet to replace it with the Rangers headgear. Many thought that only a surgical operation would prise it from him.

"You're a' set, then?" Hughie observed. Andra ignored the observation.

21

"Mine in there?", he nodded towards the bag. Hughie nodded and slumped in the chair.

"Aye," he said. "The boys are meetin' doon at McDougall's at wan o'clock."

Andra screwed his face. "That's a bit early, is it no'?"

"Well," Hughie went on, "we thought we'd meet early 'cos we'll need tae leave early. Somebody stole the bus."

Andra spluttered: "How can ye steal a bloody big bus?" he snapped angrily. "Ah'll bet it was left ootside the chapel again. That's jist askin' for it."

Hughie shrugged. "Well, you an' me wull be a' right, he said. "Big Sammy says he'll gie us a lift."

"Not on your Nellie," Andra said adamantly. "Ah am definitely no' sittin' in the back o' that hearse again. Big Sammy forgets himsel'. He gets cerried away. We ended up at Sandymount Cemetery the last time. Ah wis hivin' a kip when he woke me up. The only other bloke mair surprised than me wis that taxi driver who had drew alang side us. Naw. we'll walk."

Hughie saw the logic in Andra's outburst. "Aye, we could be buried before the kick-off," he said.

Changing the subject, Andra's eyes fell on the carry-out. Ach, let's hiv a snifter," his eyes sparkling in anticipation. "A couple o' glasses, Jean."

Jean took two whisky glasses from the cupboard and gave them a deft wipe with the tea towel. Hughie rummaged in the bag and pulled out a quarter bottle.

"Don't forget that Clarence is coming up," Jean said handing over the glasses to Andra.

"Aye, ah'll keep him some," Andra said holding the tumblers towards Hughie who poured eagerly.

"Well, I'd better get myself ready," Jean murmured and vanished into the bedroom.

"Who's Clarence?," Hughie inquired curiously.

"Well, he's no a lion at the zoo," Andra replied, taking a good swig.

"Eh?" Hughie raised his eyebrows. "Never mind," Andra said. "Cheers!" They drank and Hughie replenished the glasses.

"Aye," Andra said gleefully, "It'll be some gemme. We'll paralyse them."

22

"Ah'm no' sure," Hughie disagreed, shaking his head. "They've been playin' no' bad recently."

Andra ignored the traitorous remark: "But we ALWAYS rise tae the occasion, Hughie, ALWAYS. Aw, it'll be marvellous," he went on rubbing his hands," jist think o' the fightin' efter the gemme, Get stuck in there."

Hughie nodded: "Aye, ah've got oan ma tackity boots." He held up a foot to prove his point.

Andra nodded in approval. "Too true," he said. "Ye don't want tae hurt yer feet. Ah did that wance," he winced as he recalled. "Ah gave this bloke a good kick oan the shin an' nearly crippled masel'. The bloody swine had an ironleg. It's wis like kickin' a bloody lamp post."

Hughie nodded sympathetically: "Nae consideration, some people," he said.

"It's no' a fair world, Hughie," Andra continued, "This yin Clarence is gonny see whit real sport is the day. Whit wid you say Hughie about a bloke who drinks nuthin' but Blue Nuns?"

Hughie thought for a moment: "It's a bad habit . . . ha-ha . . . get it?"

Andra did not appreciate the joke: "Ach shut up" he snarled. It'll be somethin' stronger for us anyway." Then like a mischievous schoolboy, "Ah've goat a couple o' quid hidden in an auld cardigan for a few sherberts efter the gemme."

This surprised Hughie, "Where did ye get it?" he asked curiously."

"Ah took in washin'," Andra said. This admission stunned Hughie. He had never known Andra to toil and particularly to demean himself by such feminine pursuits.

"You took in washin'?" he uttered.

"Aye, fae a backcourt in Carntyne," Andra sniggered. "Then ah pawned it."

Both burst out laughing. Hughie re-filled the glasses and relaxed back in the chair.

"Who's this Clarence ye've been talkin' aboot?" Andra winced at the name.

"Aye, look Hughie," he said, "he's Jean's boyfriend an' he wants tae come tae the match wi' me the day. Ah don't think the boys will mind a stranger comin' wi' us, wull they?"

"So long as he's wan o' us, it disnae matter," Hughie said.

"He's comin' up tae ask ma permission," Andra went on.

"Tae go tae the match?"

"Naw . . . for Jean's haun' . . . ye know," Andra replied with irritation. "They're gettin' spliced, ye mean?"

Andra shook his head in despair: "Well, he disnae want her bloody haun jist tae scratch his back. Ye talk a lot o' crap sometimes Hughie." He explained as simply as he could. It was not one of Hughie's brighter days, he reckoned.

"He wants tae go tae the gemme wi' me . . . break the ice. Ye know whit ah mean?" Hughie was surprised. "Ah didnae know they did that these days," he said.

"Did whit?", Andra asked.

"Asked for consent tae get married," Hughie replied, "Ah mean, did YOU ask Annie's faither?"

"Naw," Andra said, his mind going back to the fateful day. "HE telt ME. He presuaded me that his Annie wis the wan for me."

"How did he persuade ye?"

"Wi a bloody big bunch o' fives," Andra answered, clenching his fist. "Mind ye, he didnae get away Scot free. He wis aff his work for three weeks efter whit he did tae me."

"Ye let him have it, Andra!" Hughie said with approval. "Naw, he broke his knuckles," Andra replied painfully. "He was a six-foot tall coalman."

"This fella Clarence," Hughie went on, "ur you gonny belt him?"

"Naw, ah'll wait an' see how he behaves at the match," Andra said. "See how he swears, an' that." Hughie shrugged, "Maybe he disnae swear," he said.

"Aw, Hughie," Andra answered incredulously, "HOW CAN WE POSSIBLY SHOUT ENCOURAGEMENT TAE THE BOYS WITHOUT SWEARIN'? It's no' possible."

"Maybe he'll no' want tae encourage them," Hughie shrugged, "Maybe he's a Pape. Whit's his second name anyway?"

THIS had never entered Andra's mind. Jean's boyfriend a CATHOLIC? The thought did not bear thinking about. Andra felt a shiver running through him. Darting quickly towards the bedroom door he said: "Ah never asked her that, hing oan." He called out in panic: "Jean . . . Jean . . . whit's Clarence's second name?"

"Burns," Jean answered.

24

Andra sighed with relief. For a moment there he had visions of being ostracised by his clan. An exclusion order from McDougall's would have been his death knell. It did not bear thinking about. Turning to Hughie, he said; "There ye are . . . a good, Scoatch name. Jist as well you thought about that, Hughie."

Hughie beamed at the compliment: "Ye must think o' everythin'. When's the weddin'?

"Give them time," Andra said. "They're no' bloody well engaged yet. Ah've still tae give ma permission."

"Aye, but if you say 'Naw', that's no gonny stoap him, is it?" said Hughie said.

Andra nodded, "Ye're dead right, Hughie. Still it gies me a chance tae size him up."

"Maybe HE wants tae size YOU up," Hughie commented. Andra had not thought of that. The idea annoyed him: "Cheeky swine," he said. "Our Jean could get anybody she fancied. That midgie man wis after her for months. Good wages, they blokes, but Jean's a bit hoyty-toyty."

The mention of money prompted Hughie to continue the subject. "It'll cost ye A FEW BOB," he said. "Whit will?" Andra wanted to know. "A weddin'," Hughie went on. "Ah mean it's the bride's folks that hiv tae spend maist o' the money . . . for the reception, an' that."

Andra shook his head: "The Brigton Public Hall'll no' cost much an' Annie's sister Cathie works in the meat market . . . they'll no' miss a pig or two. Then there's wee Jimmy at the bond, put that lot the gither an' some spuds fae the fruit market an' ye've got a meal fit for a king."

Hughie shook his head: "Ach, there's mair tae it than THAT," he said.

There was a loud rap on the door. Jean's voice called out: "I'll get it."

Andra did not agree with Hughie. There were always corners that could be cut. It just depended on knowing the right people. He remembered his own wedding.

"That's mair than Annie an' me had. A fish supper an' a boattle o' Tizer an' a night at the Geggie, that wis OOR lot. Ah'll tell ye this, Hughie . . ." Andra did not complete his sentence. Jean entered followed by a young man. Andra's mouth fell open. Hughie jumped out of his chair as though he had been stung.

25

Jean gazed lovingly into the young man's eyes: "Dad," she said, "this is Clarence."

Clarence smiled and offered his outsretched hand. He was rigged out in the green and white colours of Celtic Football Club . . . scarf, wooly hat and rosette. "Nice to meet you, Mr Thomson," he said.

Andra's roar could be heard at Bridgeton Cross. Pointing frantically at the door he bellowed: "Get him away . . . away wi' him . . . ah jist don't believe this. Hughie . . . Hughie . . . promise me that ye'll no' tell the boys," he pleaded. Hughie was rooted to the spot. His eyes stared, fixed on Clarence. He was a man mesmerised . . . stunned into rigidity. Andra shook him violently. Hughie began to gibber . . . meaningless sounds pouring from his mouth. Walking slowly as though hypnotised he looked straight ahead towards the door muttering: "Ye better get this sorted oot Andra." Turning, he said: "Ye might no' want tae go tae the match in Big Sammy's hearse, Andra. But if ye take that eejit wi' ye, ye'll definitely come back in it." And he was gone, shaking his head in disbelief.

Clarence was the first to speak: "I'm sorry if I upset you Mr Thomson," he said.

"That's a' right," Andra snapped, 'GET OOT." Jean quickly intervened. "Oh dad, it's my fault. I told Clarence that you were going to see Celtic and Rangers and that you were a devoted fan. But I didn't mention which team. He's obviously misunderstood. It's all a mistake."

"It's a mistake a' right," Andra rasped. "Tell me he's jist a mirage. Tell me he'll disappear in a minute."

Clarence took the hat from his head and pushed it deep into his pocket. "Is there any way I can make it up to you . . ." he began. Andra shook his head vehememtly: "Nuthin' short of droppin' deid will suffice," he snapped. "Get the gear aff. Ye've nearly detached ma retina."

Clarence quickly removed the scarf and rosette. Jean took them from him: "I'll put these away," she said.

"In the midden . . . in the midden," Andra hollered . . ."an' don't let anybody see ye." Jean hurriedly left the room. Andra had flopped into the chair and was cradling his head in his hands mutterring: "Ah jist canny believe this . . ."

Clarence produced a full bottle of whisky from his pocket: "I . . . er . . . I," he said shyly, "I thought you might like a wee dram before the kick-off."

The words struck Andra with missile force. He looked up, saw the bottle and was off the chair faster than a greyhound from the trap. Snatching the bottle from Clarence's outstretched hand his manner took on a more demeaning attitude:

"Well, ah do nut usually partake before the match, but as this is a special occasion . . ." he said, pouring himself a large one. "The Gers, bless 'em" he toasted.

"The 'Gers," Clarence replied pushing forward a glass and receiving a thimbleful.

Indicating a chair, Andra said: "Sit doon." Clarence accepted the invitation. Andra poured similar measures and sat opposite Clarence who sipped slowly.

"Well, " Clarence began,"I must say that was a bad start I got off to."

Andra nodded: "They don't come any badder, son." Andra downed his glass and poured a re-fill. "Drink up, drink up," he said, leaning over and adding a splash to Clarence's glass. Then, turning towards the painting of King Billy, raised his glass: "Tae King Billy an' his magnificent hoarse in that great big stable in the sky. May it crap a' ower Celtic Park during a match."

"Cheers," Clarence said uncommittedly. Andra leaned back. "Noo," he began, "ye came here tae ask me somethin' special."

"Well," Clarence said nervously. "It's . . . er . . . Jean and me. We . . . er . . . that is . . . we want to get married." Andra seemed to ponder this statement.

"Ah see, " he said, "An' dae you think you could gie her the kind of livin' whit she has been accustomed to?"

"Oh, indubitably," Clarence said, without hesitation.

"Ah had a feelin' that's whit ye would say," Andra said, knitting his brows. "Let me put it another way, d'ye think you could gie her the kind o' livin' whit she has been accustomed tae?

Clarence nodded: "There is no problem there Mr. Thomson, I graduate in a few months and besides I have a private income from my grandfather of twenty-thousand pounds a year."

Andra gulped on his drink: "He must've been a Rangers director," he exclaimed. Twenty-thousand a year . . . this bloke could be good for a "bung" now and then. Things were looking up. "Well," Andra went on, portaying the Victorian father, "ye seem well enbowelled."

Clarence smiled at the Malapropism.

27

Then, as an after thought: "Has yer granny got a wart on her bum?"

Clarence's eyebrows rose: "I beg your pardon?" Andra was disappointed. "It disnae matter . . . jist as long as ye're no' wan o' them."

"One of them?" Clarence inquired. "Aye," Andra replied, "When ye walked in the door I thought ye might be a pape." Clarence laughed: "Oh dear me no."

Andra broached the subject of religion hesitantly. Toying with his glass, he said; "Whit . . . er . . . are ye then? Presbyterian . . . Methodist . . . Church o' Scotland . . . ?"

"Oh, I'm none of those," Clarence laughed. 'This is getting awkward', Andra thought. Then a terrible thought struck him:

"Ye're no' a Pakistani, are ye?" he snapped. "Ah mean ye can get some Pakis an' ye widnae know the difference. Couldnae hiv oor Jean being conned. Ah hiv even heard o' red-headed Indians."

Clarence did not like the avenue this conversation was going down.

"I don't think it matters one way or the other what anyone is these days," he said.

"Oh but it does tae me," Andra said with conviction

"I can assure you that I am not a Pakistani," Clarence said, impatience creeping into his voice. Andra was relieved. He poured two more drinks and relaxed.

"Ah wis a bit worried there," he confided, "drink up." Clarence sipped slowly. He still had not answered Andra's question. Andra's mind was racing. If Clarence was not forthcoming there was nothing else for it but to ask him directly what his religious affiliations were.

"Whit . . . er . . . whit are ye then?" he asked directly.

"Well, if you must know," Clarence said, "I'm Jewish."

The statement hit Andra a sledgehammer blow. He jumped to his feet in anger."Ah KNEW there wis somethin' about you," he cried. "See how ye can be fooled . . . a Jew? Ye've no' even got a big konk . . . ye look jist like anybody else . . . a Jew."

"A good Jewish lad," Clarence said quietly. Andra shook his head: "Naw, naw," he said, "ah canny hiv a neutral in this house. Ye're a barbaric race."

"What do you know about the Jewish faith," Clarence said sharply. "Plenty" Andra replied, knowingly. "Youse do nut eat ham."

"What has that got to do with it?" Clarence asked in disbelief.

28

"Ah wis arrangin' tae get a couple o' pigs knocked off for the weddin', Andra said smugly, "The weddin' that wull never be."

"That's up to Jean, isn't it?" Clarence replied. Andra shook his head: "Naw, naw . . . she is nut bringin' a Jew intae MA faimly," he cried. "Look whit your crowd did tae Christ, eh?"

"That was politics," Clarence answered, "and anyway, that happened two thousand years ago."

"It disnae matter, " Andra snapped back, "He wis a good Labour man . . . a good union man. But your crowd were a' Tories. Ye had tae shut him up . . . an' look whit ye did tae Moses, eh? Ah saw the picture . . . Charleston Heston, Ah saw it a' right . . . dancin' and prancin' while he's strugglin' and staggerin' doon the mountain wi' two bloody big slabs o' rock. Nut wan o' ye oaffered tae gie him a haun'."

"With all due respect," Clarence interrupted . . . he got no further. With a dismissive wave of the hand Andra, with finality, said: "The weddin' is AFF." Clarence rose to his feet: "Well," he said, "it doesn't matter what you think. Jean and I will be married with or without your blessing."

"Like Hell ye wull." Andra snapped. Jean rushed in sobbing, She had been listening to the tenor of the conversation from behind the door. Grasping Clarence's hand, she turned to her father pleadingly: "Oh dad stop this . . ."

Before Andra could reply, Annie walked in carrying her shopping. Catching sight of Clarence, she smiled broadly: "Hello Clarence," she said, Jean's quiet sobs told her what had feared. Annie knew the reason for Clarence's visit. She knew, too, that her husband may put up obstacles "be thrawn" even if it were just to stamp his authority. But tears she would not tolerate. Turning sharply to Andra, she demanded: "Whit's goin' oan here?"

Andra pointed a shaking finger at Clarence: "Did you know that this yin's a fivety-two?"

"If ye mean that boy's Jewish, whit aboot it?" Annie hit back, folding her arms and ready for battle.

"Whit dae ye mean, 'whit aboot it' . . . d'ye hear whit ah'm sayin'? He is a bloody Israelite." Wiping her eyes, Jean said: "I don't see that it matters."

"Oh, it matters, hen, IT matters," Andra retorted. Clarence squeezed Jean's hand affectionately. Annie's eyes narrowed. Andra saw the tell-tale sign and shifted his gaze. When Annie's eyes narrowed she was about to fire a broadside.

"Of course it disnae matter," she rapped. "If it's no' Catholics, it's Pakis an if it's no' them, it's somethin' else. If it's no' your wey o' thinkin', it's wrang. Ah'm sick an' tired o' they blinkers you wear."

Andra charged back: "Whit dae ye mean? Ah'm only tryin' to protect YOUR daughter."

"OOR daughter," Annie corrected him, "has a mind o' her ain an' it's about time you realised that. She's no' a wean noo, you know. She has her ain future tae think aboot an' if Clarence is part o' that future, it's no' for you or me tae interfere."

Jean put out a hand to pacify her mother: "Mum, you'll never get through to him."

"Aye ah'll get through tae him, he's no' gonny mess up your life," Annie said sternly.

Andra threw up his hand in frustration: "You're jist gonny let this happen withoot puttin' up a fight?"

Annie glowered: "Oh, aye, ah'll put up a fight a'right but no' wi Jean. Ah've swept yer ignorance under the carpet for years an' there's many a time ah could've walked right oot that door an' left. But ah took ye for better or worse ... that was ma vows an' ah stuck tae them. But, God forgive me, ye can jist take so much."

Clarence stepped into the fray: "Mrs Thomson ...," he began. Andra cut him off: "You keep oot o' it," he said angrily, "it disnae concern you."

"Disnae concern him?" Annie said, raising her voice, "WHO does it concern?"

Andra beat his forehead with the palm of his hand "Hiv ah no' got it intae yer heid yet ... HE — IS — A — JEW," he spelled it out.

"Aye ," Annie snapped back, "an' he's a better man than you. HE hisnae asked whit YOU are. YOU are a NUTHIN' ... dae ye hear me NUTHIN'. A' you believe in is McDougall's pub an' the boys. The Good Lord himsel' wis a Jew."

"Aye, an' THEY stuck it oan HIM," Andra sneered.

"Aye, an' if there had been a pint init you would have helped them," Annie said sharply. "Naw, Andra, ye've gone too faur this time. You've ridiculed that boy. He did the gentlemanly thing comin' up here an' gein ye yer place. A' you've done is insult him." Turning to Clarence, she said: "Ah'm sorry, son."

"Whit are ye sayin' sorry tae him for?" Andra bellowed.

"Ah'm apologisin' for YOU ye ignorant get," Annie shouted angrily, "If ye were a man, ye wid apologise yersel'. But that's wan thing you've never done in your life Andra. Ye're never wrang, never YOU." Jean took her mother by the arm, "Don't upset yourself mum," she said softly.

"Never you mind, Jean," Annie said, calming herself. "Don't you worry. C'mon, we're gettin' oot o' here." Annie, still wearing her outdoor clothes turned towards the door. "There's a bad taste in ma mooth," she uttered.

"Ye must hiv ate wan o' yer ain bloody breakfasts," Andra blasted, adding . . . "Ye can come back for yer things."

Annie stormed out of the door followed by Clarence. Jean closed the door softly with one last pleading look at her father. Andra shuffled his feet uneasily. He stepped forward, "Annie" he started to say. But it was too late. Annie was gone.

CHAPTER TWO

BIG MATCH DAY

Hughie Broon turned into the street in time to see Annie and company hurry across and vanish into a closemouth. Hughie had just left McDougall's after making inquiries about the missing bus. The situation was grave . . . graver still if he and Andra had to travel in Big Sammy's hearse. He had thought about stealing a car but quickly dismissed the idea due to the fact that he could not drive. Somebody in the pub had suggested Shanks's Pony and Hughie had suggested that somebody should contact Shanks. He wondered why a ripple of laughter has swept round the pub. He had travelled by cart before and did not find the experience demeaning. Andra would figure something out, he was sure of that.

Andra hurried to answer the rapping on the door. His face fell when Hughie stepped in.

"Ah saw Annie an' Jean an' that big fella doon there," Hughie said, flopping into a chair.

"Did ye . . er . . . see whaur they went?" Andra asked being as nonchalant as he could.

"Aye . . . jist up Cathie's close acroass the road".

Andra was relieved. Annie was not too far away.

Cathie was Annie's older sister and it wasn't the first time his wife had taken refuge there after a tiff. Andra felt better at this news. He slapped his thigh.

"Right," he said, "if that's the wey she wants it let her stey there . . . let them baith stey there." Hughie's mouth fell open. "Ye . . . ye mean . . . Annie's left ye?"

"Aye," Andra said with the tone of a wronged husband, "An' for whit, eh? A fivety-two. Given up a good hame she has."

Hughie was stunned at this terrible news. "Annie's . . . Annie's . . . run away wi' a JEW?"

"Don't be stupid," Andra said with impatience. "NO Annie . . . Jean. Ye saw the big dreep."

"Aw, naw," Hughie shook his head. "That big bloke was definitely a Catholic . . . look at the gear he wis wearin'."

"God forbid . . . it's no' as bad as that," Andra said, "Naw, he's a

JEW, Hughie. How could ah ever face the boys, eh? Can ye imagine me goin' into the pub sayin' — 'This is ma son-in-law, Rabbi Burns'?"

Hughie thought it over. "It could've been worse," he decided.

"Only if he had been a Catholic JEW, Hughie," Andra replied, shivering at the thought. "How could he possibly turnoot tae be a Jew wi' a name like Clarence Burns, eh? Ah'll bet ah could do him under the Trades Description Act. An' tae think that oor Jean is gonny mairry intae that. Annie even had the cheek tae say that AH . . . ME . . . was biased. Look at me, Hughie. Dae AH look biased? Hiv ye ever KNOWN me tae biased, hiv ye?"

"Never, Hughie affirmed, "wi' the exception that ye'll no' drink Guinness."

"That disnae count," Andra waved his hand dismissively. "Ah hiv given them the best years o' ma life an' this is a' the thanks ah get."

"Ye could always get the boys tae gie him a doin'," Hughie suggested.

Andra shook his head. "Nae use, Hughie. The word would soon get around an' there's no' a furniture shoap or tailors in Glesca would gie us tick. We'd be cuttin' oor ain throats."

"Whit aboot Annie?" Hughie asked.

"Naw, Annie likes him. She would never gie him a doin', " Andra replied.

"Naw, ah mean, whit are YOU gonny dae about Annie."

Andra was silent for a moment. "Aye, Annie," he thought aloud, "Ach, she'll be back before the night's oot." Hughie arose. "Well, c'moan. It's time we were gettin' doon tae meet the boys at McDougall's . . . ye're still goin' tae the gemme, uren't ye?"

'What a stupid question', Andra thought.

"How could ah let the boys down? Wait till ah get ma cardigan," Andra said, hurrying towards the bedroom. Hughie twiddled his thumbs, eyeing up the remainder of Clarence's bottle of whisky. He jumped in fright. Andra's raging voice bellowed from the bedroom and the man himself appeared . . . empty handed.

"Ma cardigan, ma two quid . . . it's away . . . vanished . . ." Andra was distraught.

Hughie was philosophical. "The rag man wis in the street earlier."

Andra snapped his fingers. "That's it, Hughie, ah'll bet she's found the two quid an' flogged the cardigan tae the ragman." Andra was devastated.

"Ach, never mind," Hughie shrugged, "the boys'll see us a'right."

"Ah hope so, ah hope so," Andra said depressingly. Andra placed his blue and white tile hat on his head and looked approvingly at himself in the mirror, he flicked a speck of dandruff from his shoulder. He was satisfied. "C'mon, Hughie . . . oor voices are needed. The cup's waiting tae be collected — WE ARRA PEOPLE." he sang the last phrase with gusto.

Before Andra and Hughie got to the door Annie, Jean and Clarence walked in.

"A-HA," Andra exclaimed, "ye came back, eh?" Annie ignored him and walked straight past.

"Aye," she said, "for ma things."

Andra shrugged. "Aye, well ah canny wait. Ah hiv got a hearse tae catch."

"Nae such luck," Annie retorted."

Andra and Hughie left and their bellowing of "We Arra People" could be heard echoing down in the closemouth

"Well, that's him oot the road," Annie commented.

"Are you sure you're doing the right thing, mum?" Jean asked with concern. "You know what dad's like." Nobody had to tell Annie what Andra was like. She knew the right strategy.

"Don't worry aboot anythin'," she said. "Yer faither's a bigot, Jean, but he's no' a REAL bigot, if ye know whit ah mean. He THINKS he is . .. but there's a loat of good in him as well as his faults."

"I'm sorry I've caused all this trouble," Jean said sadly. "Me too," Clarence added.

"Don't any of ye be sorry," Annie said, "Andra would've found fault no matter who Jean would've wanted tae mairry."

"What will we do?" Jean asked, dumped.

"We'll stey wi' yer Auntie Cathy. HE'LL ask me back first . . . you mark ma words." Annie knew her husband.

"And if he doesn't?" Jean said.

"He'll starve tae death. He'll know who his pals are then," Annie replied, "If he thinks Willie Waddell's gonny send him up a tightner, he's in for a shock," Annie laughed.

Clarence had been thinking the situation over. "Do you think it would make any difference if he met my folks?" he asked, "I mean, dad's a man of the world. He knows how to handle situations like this."

Annie's eyes lit up. "That just might be a good idea, Clarence," she agreed.

Jean was dismayed at the thought. "Oh, we couldn't ask your parents to come up here!" she exclaimed.

Annie was annoyed at her daughter's remarks.

"And why not," she demanded, "There's nuthin' tae be ashamed of livin' in Brigton. We didnae a' get the chances in life."

Jean was contrite immediately. "Oh Mum, I didn't mean that . . . I mean . . ."

Annie did not allow her to finish the sentence. "Yer granny reared ten weans here an' they never wanted for a bite. Even durin' the bad years you could've ate yer dinner aff the linoleum." Then, thoughtfully: "Ah suppose it's only right that ye want tae better yersel'. Ah must admit ah am lookin' forward tae a hoose wi' a bath an' a toilet in it . . . wan o' they high flats that are springin' up. An if ah get the chance tae move in, ah'm gonny ask for the twenty-fifth flair," she laughed.

"Oh, that's awful high," Jean exclaimed. Annie giggled. "No high enough," she sniggered. "Ah'll make sure the lifts are aff when yer faither gets hame. If he's drunk when he arrives at the close, he'll be sober by the time he gets up tae the hoose."

They all laughed.

"In that case, you'll never see him," Jean said.

"That's another good point in their favour," Annie giggled . . . "Noo, Clarence, aboot yer mither an faither . . .?"

"Dad's a pretty astute man," Clarence said. "He'll handle things all right."

"Oh, Andra jist isnae THINGS," Annie said. "He's the bionic man as faur as he's concerned. He's got a bionic throat anyway . . . he keeps it well oiled." Everybody laughed.

"Well, I think this meeting is going to be a disaster," Jean said with a grimace.

"Don't you worry aboot anythin', Jean. Ah hiv a feelin' yer faither is gonny get his cummuppance," Annie said, "C'mon noo, let's get oor things." Annie walked over to the painting of King Billy and stared at it for a moment. "It's aboot time you had some competition", she said. "YOU and your cuddy."

Suddenly there was loud neighing of a horse. Annie jumped with fright clutching her heart. Then a voice rasped from the street below

... "RAGS. Any Ole Rags ..."

"Oh, it's the bloomin' ragman," she said with relief. The horse neighed once more as Annie, Clarence and Jean closed the door behind them.

McDougall's was bursting at the seams. The bus had not been found and there was consternation amongst the revellers. Big Sammy had already drawn up his hearse outside the doors but had no takers. He knew to wait. John Barleycorn would nudge some business his way when the time was ripe. Sammy was an astute and patient man.

Andra and Hughie had pushed their way to the bar and were refreshing themselves.

McDougall lifted their glasses and wiped the bar. "How's it gon', Andra?" he inquired.

"Could'nae be better," Andra said, taking a swig.

"Ah thought ah saw your Jean wi' a big Celtic supporter the day" McDougall said. "Has she chinged her allegiance?" he laughed.

"Aw, him," Andra said awkwardly. "Naw, ye've been seein' things. That's her boyfriend. He's a ... er ... bus driver. That's their new uniform. Ah don't think much o' them masel ... maybe it's becuase he's oan the PRIESThill route ... eh?" Andra laughed.

"Aye, or BISHOPbriggs", McDougall laughed.

McDougall left to attend to impatient shouts from the other end of the counter. He was still laughing.

'That's a point," Hughie said, "Whit team DAE Jews support?"

"Ah don't think they support any," Andra said. "They're no' really up on the fitba' scene.

"Ah've seen some at Firhill," Hughie said.

"Well, that jist proves ma point doesn't it," Andra answered, taking a swig.

Their conversation was interrupted by a thumping at the other end of the bar calling for attention. The babble died down.

"Boys," a voice said. "We hiv been generously gied a bus for oor use today by the local Celtic Supporters Association who heard of oor plight. A round of applause fur their sportin' gesture." The bar erupted into rapturous clapping. Only Andra didn't join in in the appreciation. He clouted Hughie on the wrist for daring to include himself in the gratitude.

"Whit dae ye think you're doin'"? he snapped.

"Well, that wis helluva good o' them," Hughie replied sulkily, rubbing his wrist.

"Ur ye daft?" Andra snapped, "D'you really think that bus wull ever see Hampden?"

"Ah don't see why not'," Hughie said.

"Ah'm tellin' ye that bus wull no' even see the other side of the Jamaica Bridge . . . an' it widnae surprise me if the seats wiz wired. Ye'll a' end up like a bus load o' Golden Wonder crisps."

Hughie didn't think the Celtic fans would go THAT far to reduce the volume of the Rangers support. But decided that he'd better keep his mouth shut.

McDougall's began to empty quickly as the fans trooped out to the waiting bus, singing their songs lustily. Hughie made to leave but Andra pulled him back. "Finish yer drink," he said. "We'll make oor ain wey there."

"No' goin' oan the bus?" McDougall inquired, as he cleared away empty glasses.

"That is a Chariot of Fire oot there," Andra replied, "widnae sit in it in an asbestos suit."

"Ach, ye're haverin'," McDougall said, wiping a table. "It's an auld bus it'll get them there an' back an' that's the main thing."

"Aye, if they're lucky," Andra said, draining his glass . . . "C'mon, Hughie."

Hughie hastily finished his drink and the two men walked out into the street. The bus was ready to pull away and was ringing with the chants and songs of the happy supporters.

"TRAITORS," Andra bawled as the bus departed and vanished round the corner, the chorus echoing in the distance.

"Wis that a shamrock painted oan the bus?" Hughie inquired.

"The whole thing's a bloody sham," Andra snorted. A toot of a car horn grabbed their attention. Big Sammy was sitting in his hearse, drumming his fingers on the steering wheel and whistling softly.

"C'mon, Hughie," Andra turned towards the parked hearse, with Hughie running behind him.

"Ye're no' goin' in THAT, are ye?"

"Hughie," Andra groaned, "it's either that or we'll be hearin' the final whistle fae Paisley Road Toll. Noo, c'mon."

Andra adjusted his blue and white tile hat and gave his rickety a vigorous twirl, making sure it was tuned up. Big Sammy rolled down the window on the passenger side of his vehicle. "You boys want a lift?"

"We would gladly partake of your kind oaffer if ye wull extend tae us the courtesy of credit."

"Whit does that mean, Andra?" Hughie asked.

"It means we're skint, Hughie."

"Ah've got a few quid, Andr. . ." Hughie got a quick dig in the ribs. Andra was well acquainted with Hughie's financial status. That cash would be their means of a liquid celebration after "the boys" had picked up the cup.

"Ah could maybe dae a deal wi' ye," Big Sammy said, scratching his cheek thoughtfully.

"Whit is it?" Andra inquired.

"See that bloke in the back there?"

It was the first time Andra had noticed that a coffin was laid out in the back of the hearse.

Hughie also noticed and felt his legs buckle slightly.

"That . . . that's a coaffin, Andra," he stammered.

"It's no' oor cairry-oot, Hughie, that's for sure."

Hughie shivered. "Is there somebody in it . . . deid?"

"Naw, we're gonny smuggle him intae the gemme . . . he hisnae got a ticket. Noo shut up Hughie."

Big Sammy interrupted. "Ah've got tae drap him oaf at the Co-op parlour an' if you boys gie me a haun' ah'll take ye oan tae the gemme. Fair enough?"

"Fair enough," Andra beamed, climbing into the car followed by a Hughie who was trying not to glance into the back.

Hughie sat with his eyes tightly closed during the short journey. It did not take long to arrive at the parlour. Big Sammy stubbed out his cigarette and indicated that Andra should do the same. There were still a few good puffs left and Andra deftly nipped his cigarette and stuck the butt in his jacket pocket. The men clambered out of the cab.

"You two get him oot, wull ye? An' ah'll see tae the business," Big Sammy said, fumbling through some official looking papers.

Hughie did not approve of this at all but knew better than to comment. Andra had no hesitation. Opening the rear doors of the hearse, he called to Hughie, who was dallying . . . "You get in there an' gie it a shove," he ordered. Before Hughie could object, he was hauled up by the collar and thrust into the hearse.

"Noo shove," Andra said.

Hughie pushed with all of his might and was relieved to find that the coffin glided easily out of the back doors. The two men manhandled the casket as best they could, Hughie staggering uncontrolably under the weight. Big Sammy, finding the street doors of the parlour closed, had vanished around the back of the building. Andra and Hughie were left standing on the pavement with their charge.

"Andra, if ye don't put this doon ah am gonny hiv a rupture," Hughie groaned.

"Staun' it up here against the wa'," Andra puffed.

They struggled across the pavement, groaning under the weight, and gradually managed to stand the coffin upright, one on either side to keep it balanced.

"Don't let any dugs near it," Andra said, "hiv some dignity."

Andra re-lit his cigarette butt and was glad of the rest. He flicked a speck of ash from his rosette and gave his rickety another twirl, making sure it was still in good working order. He wondered why people were giving him glances as they passed by but assumed they were quite taken by his tile hat and other colourful paraphernalia. Big Sammy was taking his time and Hughie began to worry at the delay.

"Ah wonder who's in there," Andra said curiously, nodding towards the coffin.

"Ah heard Bowly McGeachie wisnae keepin' well," Hughie volunteered.

"Naw, it widnae be Bowly," Andra said, shaking his head, "they'll need tae bury him in a bloody barrel." The big, stern-faced, cop was beside them before they noticed his approach.

"Whit's goin' on here, then?" he growled. "Ah take it ye're goin' tae a funeral?"

"Aye," Andra said, taking another drag at his butt . . ."Celtic's."

Hughie giggled. The policeman wasn't amused. Who's this, then?" he said, nodding towards the coffin.

"That's the ref," Andra answered, "we're gien him a lift."

"Funny man, eh?

Hughie did not like the way the conversation was going and had visions of them both being boxed up and missing the match.

"We . . . er . . . are jist waitin' for the undertaker tae open this door," he explained nervously. "We wiz jist gien him a haun'."

"Aye, well ye canny staun' in the pavement wi' a coaffin. So get it back in that hearse," the big cop indicated with his thumb. Hughie looked at Andra in dismay. He was just getting his breath back after the struggle. Hughie and Andra manhandled the heavy weight over to the hearse, watched by the policeman. After a brief struggle they managed to get it horizontal in its rightful place. Andra leaned back and mopped his brow.

"Right," the cop said, "see that it steys there." Andra turned to Hughie. "This is bloody ridiculous." he said. "We start oot for the match an' a good stiff drink. We hivnae seen the match, an' hivnae got a drink. A' we've got's the stiff."

"Aye, Big Sammy's got a lot tae answer for," Hughie commented.

Andra was getting impatient. Buses were passing packed with fans heading for the game. Blue and white scarves billowed from the open windows and the raucous singing and hand-clapping chants of the euphoric supporters only made him more distraught. Suddenly he made his mind up. "Right, Hughie, enough's enough. Big Sammy's at it. C'mon, gie me a haun' wi' this bloke in the boax."

Two doors down from the funeral parlour was the ubiquitous Indian restaurant . . . packed with diners enjoying the cut-rate "businessman's lunch."

Andra and Hughie dragged the coffin across the pavement. "You wait here," Andra said. Pushing his head through the door of the restaurant, he hollered for all to hear: "MEAT DELIVERY."

"Very good please," an Indian voice replied. "Bring it in here please."

"Right, Hughie . . . in there wi' it." The two men hauled the coffin inside and stood it up inside the entrance . . . and left hurriedly. Forks stopped abruptly in mid-air and mouths fell open. Andra and Hughie were well down the road by now and lost in the crowd.

"Let big Sammy get oot o' that," Andra laughed — "no' tae mention that bloody restaurant owner."

The two men giggled mischievously.

Supporters buses were still speeding towards Hampden Park with their noisy cargoes. Andra and Hughie waved their colours at each bus in the hope that one driver might take pity on their plight and stop. And one did. The door opened and a voice called: "Ur yez goin' tae the match?"

"Whit dae ye think we're doin . . . canvassing for the Tory Party?"

Andra replied facetiously.

"Get in," the man said and didn't have to repeat himself. Andra and Hughie clambered aboard and, profusely thanking the singing fans, made their way to the back where a couple of empty seats were just waiting to be filled.

Settling in, Andra said, "Well, Hughie . . . we ur on oor way . . . tae a massacre.

Then the duo joined in the singing with gusto.

Peter had been sitting studying all day . . . glad of the quietness. Glancing at the mantleshelf clock, he sighed. Andra would soon be returning and Peter had a good idea in what state. He did not have long to wait. A key went in the lock and Andra and Hughie were talking loudly. Andra entered and flopped into the chair. Surprisingly he was fairly sober. He didn't notice his son sitting at the table, books spread out, thinking deeply

"There's nae doot aboot it, we wis robbed," Andra complained.

Hughie shrugged: "Ye canny say two each wis a bad score."

"It should've been ten nuthin' for the boys. Ah'm tellin ye, Hughie, that ref wis biased,"

"Whit makes ye think that?" Hughie asked.

"Ma EYES, Hughie. Did ye no' watch him, eh?

"Naebody'll convince me that his whistle wisnae attached tae the end o' a rosary. When Celtic scored their first goal he couldna' stoap dancin'."

"Ach," Hughie said, "he wis jist jumpin' up tae catch the players' attention an' signalin' it wis a goal."

"Well, it had a' the movements o' an Irish jig, if ye ask me," Andra said.

Peter ignored this conversation, just glad that his father had not noticed him.

Too late! "Ah, hello son," Andra said turning. "Ah didnae see ye there. We wis busy post mortemin' the gemme."

"Whit are ye doin', Peter? Hughie asked interestedly.

"Studying."

Hughie was all for it. "That's the stuff, son. There's nuthin tae beat education."

Andra was not interested. "Ach, ye should hiv been at the gemme," he said snidely, "magic, it wis." Hughie nodded. "A hope we dae

41

better at the replay," he said.

Andra agreed with his friend's statement. "Definitely," he said . . . "an' ah hope they find the bloody bus by then. Y'know, Hughie, Ah'm, sure ah saw it at Hampden wi' King Billy's boady rubbed aff an' the Lone Ranger's painted in its place."

"Ah widnae put it past them," Hughie agreed.

"If we had put a few mair past them the day there widnae hiv tae be a replay," Andra mooted.

"Ach well it gies us a chance tae relive it a' ower again," Hughie said happily.

Andra nodded. "We'll slaughter them . . . providin' they get another ref," he said, once again quietly cursing the referee.

"Aye," Hughie said, not so much in agreement as not wanting to involve himself with Andra in a debate he knew he could not win.

"Anyway," he went on, "ah'll hiv tae go." Turning at the door, he said, "Ah'll gie ye a shout . . . an' Peter, you stick in there son."

There was a heavy silence in the room. Andra stood up, walked over to the window and looked out before returning to his seat.

Ah suppose ye know that yer mither's away . . . an' Jean as well?"

Peter nodded. "Ah met Jean in the chip shop."

"Goin' tae mairry a Jew, so she is," Andra said hoping Peter would be an ally.

"So, what's up wi' that?" Peter shrugged.

"Aw, don't YOU start," Andra sniped."

There was another short silence. Peter tidied his books and stood up.

"You know what's happening to you, don't you?" he said, turning to his father.

"Whit dae ye mean? Andra snapped, "there's nuthin' happenin' tae me."

"Oh aye there is," Peter said, pushing his point. "Your wee, bigoted world is beginning tae crack. Can you no' see that? Your wife's away, your daughter's away . . . and," he said quietly, "soon I hope to be away". Andra stared at him, "Whit d'ye mean?"

Peter shook his head. "Well, I suppose you're as well to know now than later."

"Know WHIT?" Andra cried.

"Ah told you ah was taking exams?"

"Aye, well ..." Andra's brows were knitted deeply. There was a pause, then Peter continued: "Well," he said quietly, "if ah pass, ah'll be enterin' the church ... I'm taking the cloth."

Andra stared straight ahead. He was stunned. This was a hammer blow he never expected. HIS Peter entering the church. Taking the collar. His mind swam in disbelief. Peter had not intended to tell his father his plans until after his exams and the results known. But the turn of events in the Thomson household had decided him to inform Andra and "get it out of the way."

"You had to know sometime," he said.

Andra found his voice at last. "Bu ... but ... ye canny dae that," he stammered, "Ah wanted ye tae be a plumber."

"It's what ah want, dad," Peter said with irritation.

Andra was dumbfounded at the news. "Son," he said in disbelief. "Ah never knew ye had it in ye. Ye never let oan."

"Ah've been studying for a year for these exams," Peter said.

Andra shook his head, "A' that time, eh? Ah thought ye were studyin' the racin' form."

It suddenly occurred to Andra that Peter's vocation might be no bad thing. It's not every family that has a minister in its house. Ministers have good connections. Every Masonic and Orange Lodge has its man of the cloth. Andra could see doors suddenly being opened to him, paths smoothed. Who would dare reject the father of a minister? Unexpectedly, a whole new world had opened up for him. The sting of the Hampden draw was suddenly dulled and his depression smoothed.

Andra took Peter by the shoulders. "Ma Peter ... a man o' the cloth! Who would ever hiv thought that? Think oan it, son, you could even become a Moderator. This deserves a celebration."

Andra hurried to the sideboard and produced a bottle of whisky and two glasses.

"Ah've been savin' this for a special occasion," he said pouring liberally. "As ah will not be openin' it for Jean's weddin' whit could be mair special than this, eh?

They toasted and Andra refilled the glasses. "Tae think a son o' mine is becomin' a minister ... ah jist canny get ower it. Cheers!"

"Dad," Peter said quietly, "you ... you're making a big mistake."

"Nae mistake, son." Andra interrupted, "here's tae yer holy future."

"Dad, listen to me," Peter said, just as Andra was about to gulp his measure down. "I'm going into the PRIESTHOOD — I'm going to be a PRIEST."

Andra's drink stood halfway to his mouth . . . frozen in mid-air.

"I've been trying to tell you," Peter said almost in a whisper.

The full impact of what Peter had said suddenly hit Andra. He gulped down the drink and clutching his heart, staggered towards the settee. He collapsed, gasping. Peter rushed to his aid but Andra waived him off.

"Don't talk tae me," he groaned, "don't touch me . . . a priest? . . . Aw my God . . . a priest! Ah'll never live it doon . . . never be able tae go tae Ibrox again . . . whit are ye doin' tae me? Is it blood ye want? Aw, ah'm dyin' . . . snuffin' it wi' a broken heart . . ." Peter wasn't sure if his father was acting or not. He knew that the news would shock him but he never expected this outburst of dramatics.

Turning towards the door, he said: "I'll get the doctor." The word "doctor" made Andra sit up."Naw, naw," he called "get yer mither . . . ower at Cathie's quick . . . quick . . . before ah go an' join King Billy's hoarse . . ."

Peter hurried from the house.

Immediately Peter had left, Andra jumped from the couch and poured himself a large whisky. Gulping it down, he replenished it at once. Walking over to the picture of King Billy, he stared in silence. Then, in an outburst, shook his fist. "Where wis you when a' this wis happenin', eh? Ye must've seen that he was bein' brainwashed. Ye could've at least had a word wi' somebody up there . . . John Knox or somebody. Noo ye've loast wan o' yer ain tae the other side. Ah taught him everything a son should know . . . should learn fae his faither . . . how tae swear in four languages in case we wis travellin' tae Europe wi' the boys. How tae strap a boattle inside yer leg when goin' tae the match . . . or better still, take Bowly McGeachie wi' ye an' ye could get two boattles in."

He shook his head in anguish. "How could ye let this happen?" Andra was near to tears.

Hearing voices coming from the stairhead, Andra gulped down his drink and almost flew to the couch where he lay moaning. "Aw, ah'm dyin'," he groaned. "Ah'm dyin'. Annie hurried to his side. "There, there, noo . . . you're a'right." There was genuine concern in her voice.

"You must've knew aboot this," he scolded his wife. "It wis you

44

that put the idea o' bein' a turncoat in Peter's heid."

Annie shook her head. "It wis his ain idea," she said. "He must've had it in him."

"Ye've killed me," Andra sighed, "jist like ye murdered me wi' yer bare hauns."

Peter stood and watched his father's act, convinced now that he was putting on an Oscar winning performance. Annie turned to him. "Peter, away doon an' get Mister Brown the minister. If yer faither's dyin' he'll need a' the help he can get at the ither side."

"Ah don't need a bloody minister," Andra argued, propping himself up on one elbow. And then, as an afterthought: "It's a wonder ye're no' sendin' for the rabbi."

Annie flushed. "You keep Clarence oot o' this. Even oan yer death bed ye've got a twisted, bigoted mind."

"BIGOTED", Andra hollered, "ME BIGOTED. Ah am nut wan bloody bit bigoted, ah keep tellin' ye that . . . YOU BRAINWASHED PETER."

"Naw ah didnae," Annie snapped back. "Peter asked me if he could join ma church. Ah didnae bother at first but he kept at me an' ah saw that he wis serious . . . so ah helped him. Times are chingin', Andra, ye canny stoap Peter and Jean goin' their ain wey. Clarence is a good boy."

"Clarence . . ." Andra winced.

"Aye, Clarence," Annie said. "There's a loat o' lassies jist don't bother gettin' married these days. You jist leave them alane tae get oan wi' it. Peter sits his exams next week for the seminary an' you better keep yer nose oot o' things or ye're gonny hiv nae family left." There was a moment's silence. Then Andra said quietly: "He might fail."

"It's YOU that's failed," Annie hit back. Then changing the tenor of the conversation, "Ah lit a caunle for you the day, Andra."

"Ah thought ma bloody ears were burnin'," Andra cried, clapping his hands over his ears and grimacing.

Annie stroked Andra's hair in an unusual outward sign of affection. "Here," she said softly, "let me get ye a wee dram tae calm yer nerves."

"How could ye possibly think that ah could drink at a time like this?" he uttered, shaking his head.

"Oh, well, a' right, then," Annie said.

"Well, maybe jist a wee wan," Andra piped in quickly. Annie poured him a large whisky and Andra downed it in one go. Smacking his lips, he said, "That's better." Then, taking Annie's hand, he asked pleadingly, "Ur ye comin' back tae me?"Annie shook her head. "Ah don't think so, Andra, ye hivnae chinged."

"We've had no' a bad life together, Annie."

"It's been hard Andra," Annie replied, a faraway look in her eye.

There was a long silence. Andra knew what Annie was thinking. He didn't blame her. He knew that he wasn't the easy person to live with.

Annie broke the silence. "Ah'll come back oan wan condition."Andra's eyes lit up. "Whit's that?" he asked hopefully.

"Ye'll agree tae meet Clarence's folks," Annie said.

"NEVER", Andra said with finality in his voice.

"See, there ye go again," Annie's voice rose: "Whit herm can it dae? Are ye FRIGHTENED tae meet them?"

"ME? Ah am frightened o' nuthin' an' naebody," Andra said with bravado.

"Well, whit hiv ye got tae lose, then?" Annie said, adding: "Ah've already invited them up anywey."

"Ah," Andra mocked, "so ye WIS comin' back?"

"Whether you're here or no', ah would like to meet them," Annie said, puncturing that argument: "Wull ye see them?"

Andra thought it over for a minute. Doctor's, too, have many contacts.

"Ah'll consider it," he said finally. "When ur they comin' up?"

"Wednesday night," Annie said.

"Wednesday night?", Andra shook his head. "Impossible. that's the replay night. If ah didnae turn up the boys would be wonderin'. Ah couldnae say it was because ah wis hivin' a Jewish doactor up for tea . . . it's oot the question."

"Please yersel'", Annie said, "but ah'll be here tae make them welcome. You'll only show yer ignorance if ye're no' here."

"Ye can dae whit ye like," Andra cried, "but ah'll tell ye this, Jean wull mairry Clarence ower ma deid body."

"So, ye'll no' be here, then, is that whit ye're sayin'?" Annie asked with nonchalance.

"Well . . . er . . ." Andra stammered, not wanting to show weakness but, at the same time, thinking of the opportunities he might miss by being aquainted with a doctor. "You'd better make it efter the match . . . efter the gemme."

"An' you better be oan yer best behaviour," Annie warned, "Ah don't want a red face an' neither does Jean."

Andra ignored the remark.

"Ah'll jist hiv a man-tae-man talk with this bloke an' if he gets me tae chinge ma mind, Ah wull tear up ma season ticket tae Ibrox," he said smugly.

"Is that a bet?" Annie asked.

"Ah swear oan King Billy's hoarse", Andra said, holding up his hand in a mock oath, "May it hiv diarrhoea ower Ibrox Park if ah am nut tellin' the truth."

At that moment Peter hurried in followed be a clergyman. Andra lay back on the couch groaning . . . "Ah'm dyin', ah'm dyin'," he gasped.

"Sorry I took so long," Peter said, breathlessly. "Ah couldn't get Mr. Brown. This is Father Brogan . . ." Andra's blood zoomed up a hundred points. His face purple, he raised himself up. "FATHER Brogan," he yelled . . . "Oh, God . . . ah'm surrounded . . . ah'm surrounded."

o o o o o O O O O O o o o o o

There was a heavy atmosphere in the Thomson house over the following days. Annie and Jean had moved back. Annie had been affronted at the reception Andra had given to the young Father Brogan and she didn't let Andra forget it. "Ignorant get," she said, 'treating a priest like that."

"It wisnae MA fault," Andra answered, "When he asked me if ah wanted the last rites, ah thought he meant ma congugals — how wis ah supposed tae know whit he meant? A' ah said wis that ah didnae think you were up tae it."

Wednesday had come around — replay night — and Andra had his tile hat suitably dusted down and was ready for action. He had just been down to McDougall's to make sure transport to Hampden Park had been acquired. Assured that it had been he returned home to collect his gear. Peter was hard at his studies when Andra walked in.

"Is HE still here?" he sneered. "Nae shame in him. Look at him . . . sittin' under ma photie o' King Billy."

"Never you mind him Peter," Annie said. "The hoarse is constapatit," she knew how Andra's mind worked.

"Ma heart can hardly take this," Andra said, clutching his chest. "It's sacriligous."

"Heart lazy, that's your problem," Annie sniped. "Ye've been moanin' a' week aboot yer heart . . . but there's nuthin' wrang wi' yer appetite."

"Cos ah'm gettin' starved," Andra moaned. "Black bloody puddin' every day. See, if ah ever need a transfusion they'll no' send tae the blood bank, they'll send tae the bloody butchers."

"There'll be nothin' wrang wi' yer heart tonight," Annie remarked sarcastically.

A surge of euphoria swept through Andra at the thought. "Ah'll jist hiv tae take the chance that it disnae pack in during' the excitement," he said. "Ah'll be there . . . even if it means crawlin' oan ma hauns an' knees."

"That's usually the wey ye come back," Annie said. Andra ignored the remark and turned his attention once more on Peter .

"Look," he said, "can ye no' take yer books somewhere else . . . like the barras or somethin' . . .? Peter glanced up but said nothing. He continued with his swotting. It was too much for Andra. Hurrying over, he snatched his coveted painting from the wall saying "This is nae place for you." He vanished into the bedroom, the painting under his arm.

"Don't you worry aboot him, son," Annie said almost apologetically.

"Ach, ah'm used to it now," Peter replied without looking up.

A roar of rage from the bedroom made Annie jump. Andra came storming into the room clutching Annie's precious picture of the Pope.

"Whit the hell's THIS?" he screamed. "It is blasphemous, that's whit it is. For a minute there they wis lyin' side-by-side under the bed . . . Good King Billy an' the Pope."

Annie had kept the Pope's picture out of sight but now and then, when she was alone, she would bring it to the surface for "a wee blether."

Andra threw the picture to the floor. "Here, hiv ah been lyin' on top o' him a' these years?" he demanded.

"Never you mind," Annie said angrily, retrieving the painting and lovingly wiping it with her apron.

"Nae wonder ah've got a bloody sore back," Andra groaned, "he's been lyin' there laughin' up his bloody habit at me."

"That is Good Pope John," Annie said, . . . "a gentleman."

"Well, you get him oot o' this hoose jist as fast as ye like," Andra ordered, "There's only wan John gonny hing in these wa's an' that's Good John Greig. You get rid o' Gunga Din here or there'll be trouble."

Peter threw down his pen in disgust and turned to his father. "Who do you think YOU are?" he said trying to contain his anger. "Why should mum not be allowed tae . . ."

"Leave it be," Annie interrupted, not wanting her son to get himself into deeper water with his father.

"Aye, YOU mind yer ain business," Andra snapped, "HE is gonny be YOUR boss anywey, int he?"

Andra hurried back into the bedroom and could be heard saying: "Sorry, your majesty . . . ah didnae know he wis there."

Annie placed the picture of Pope John in the top drawer of the sideboard with the comment — "It'll just be for a wee while, yer Holiness. Ah can proamise ye that." Peter shook his head and continued with his studies. Andra re-entered and flopped on to the couch.

"You got rid o' him?" he said.

"For the time being'," Annie replied.

"Jist as long as ah'm no' sittin' on top o' him . . . a pain in the back's bad enough."

"Ye already are a pain in the erse anyway, so it widnae make any difference," Annie retorted.

Andra ignored the remark but had a quick look under the cushion to satisfy himself. Annie took her coat from behind the door and adjusted her headscarf.

"Ah'm, away doon tae the shoaps," she said, turning, "see if ye can keep oot o' trouble till ah get back," she threw Andra a scornful glance and left.

Andra lit a cigarette and leaned back, closing his eyes. Where had he gone wrong, he wondered? Peter had always seemed a sensible enough boy except he didn't like football. Andra could never understand that. It wasn't natural in his way of thinking. He had never shown any inclination towards the pious life — never ate fish on a Friday. As far as Jean was concerned, she obviously needed new

49

contact lenses. He sighed a deep sigh and turned to Peter, who was swotting away at the kitchen table.

"Can ah dae anythin' tae make ye chinge yer mind?" Andra asked hopefully.

Peter shook his head. "Nothing!"

Could ye no' jist be a minister?" Andra pleaded, "Ah mean it's the same uniform, int it . . . same collar." Peter looked up. "Don't be silly," he said. "It's whit's behind the collar."

"It's a bloody hard neck that's behind yours," Andra snapped. "There'll be nae gimp, ye know," he added, "nane o' that. "He crooked his arm.

"There's more to life than THAT!"

"It's no' natural," Andra said dolefully.

A sharp knock on the door ended the scene. Andra struggled up from the couch and answered. He returned followed by Hughie, who was carrying a parcel.

"Are ye up?" Hughie inquired of Andra.

"Naw, ah usually sleep staunin' up like this," Andra said sarcastically.

Hughie let the remark go and pulled a bottle from his parcel.

"Ah thought ye might like a wee belt tae cheer ye up — put some life intae ye," he said smiling. Andra's eyes lit up. "Ah could be doin' wi' a drink," he said, producing a couple of glasses from the sink. Andra poured two large ones and Hughie toasted. "May the boys dae well the night," he said cheerfully.

"It'll be a massacre," Andra said. Hughie sat down on the easy chair while Andra poured another couple.

"Ah, ye're still at it," Hughie said, noticing Peter at work. "Good on ye, son . . . er whit actually are ye doin'?"

Peter slowly placed his pen on the table. "Ah'm takin' the cloth, Hughie."

Andra spluttered and jumped between the two, topping up Hughie's glass until it spilled over.

"Aye . . . he's . . . er . . . takin' up tailorin'", he quickly chipped in.

Hughie was surprised at Andra's sudden generosity with the drink . . . even if he did supply it.

"A good trade, that," he said nodding.

"Ah'll be saving souls," Peter added, a wry smile on his face.

50

"He's doin' a bit o' cobblin' oan the side," Andra put in quickly, refilling Hughie's glass once more.

"It's good tae be enterprisin', Peter," Hughie said in admiration.

"Hughie," Peter went on enjoying his father's frustration, "ah'm taking Holy Orders."

"He's goin' messages for the meenister, Hughie, his housekeeper's sick," Andra said abruptly, scowling at Peter.

"That's nice," Hughie said innocently.

"Dad, you're fightin' a losing battle," Peter said. "Why don't ye just accept things? Ah really hope ah get assigned to this parish . . . that'll bring ye doon from yer bigoted pedestal."

Hughie's eyebrows shot up. "Parish? Whit parish? . . . whit does he mean, Andra?"

"He means Social Security Oaffice, Hughie, that's whit they call it noo. It's . . . er . . . a civil service joab . . . aye, that's whit it is . . . a civil service joab." Andra said, mopping his brow.

"Ah didnae know the civil service dealt wi' suits an' cobblers an' that," Hughie muttered, "no' tae mention going' messages for the minister."

Peter rose slowly walked over to the sideboard and returned with Annie's picture of Pope John in his hand. He held it up for all to see. Hughie froze, glass midway to his mouth.

"This man, Hughie, will be ma boss," Peter said defiantly.

Hughie turned to Andra. "But that's . . . that's," he stammered.

"Mike Yarwood, Hughie, bloody Mike Yarwood the impersonator . . . anybody can bloody well see that," Andra blurted out, grabbing the picture and depositing it back in the sideboard drawer and out of sight. Hughie was not convinced. "Whis that no' the . . . the . . . Pope?" He found it difficult to say the word.

"Aye, it was," Peter said. "Pope John, it was, an' ah'm joinin' his flock."

Andra cradled his head in his hands.

"Ye mean . . . ye mean . . . ." Hughie started.

"Calm doon, Hughie, jist calm doon," Andra said, finding his voice. "It jist means Peter is goin' up tae the Campsies tae dae a bit o' shepherdin' . . . ."

"It means ah'm becomin' a PRIEST, Hughie . . . a priest . . . a CATHOLIC PRIEST," Peter said with finality. Andra gazed up at the

51

ceiling to make sure it was still there. The roof amazingly had not collapsed. He looked at Hughie, whose mouth was wide open, and threw his arms up in the air despairingly. The game was up. McDougall's would have a whip round for a new shroud for him. The bloke they had dumped at the Indian Restaurant was a far luckier man than he was. Andra flopped on to the couch. Hughie spoke first. "Andra . . .?" he looked at his bosom pal with pity.

"Ah canny believe it masel'," Andra said, shaking his head. "Noo ye know . . . it's been happenin' right under ma ain roof an' ah never suspected."

"It's like the plague has come, int it?" Hughie said sadly. "Ah mean, ye could take that big Jewish bloke intae McDougall's tae meet the boys . . . but a PRIEST?"

"Aye . . . a hauf wi' a dash o' holy watter," Andra said, shivering at the thought. Turning to Hughie, he said quietly, "Ah suppose ye'll be tellin' the boys the night?"

"The boys . . . the boys," Peter said angrily . . . "that's a' you ever worry about." Peter stormed out of the room, slamming the door behind him.

Andra and Hughie stood in silence. Andra poured another couple of drinks. This was the lowest point in his life. He raised his glass. "Wull ye?" he asked Hughie.

"Will a whit?"

"Be tellin' the boys the night?"

"It widnae be fair no' tae," Hughie said, his allegiance between Andra and the boys suddenly being put to the test. Andra knew that Hughie was right. "Ah understaun'," he said, "Ah mean . . . well . . . they would feel uncomfortable, ye know."

"Aye," Hughie agreed. "Staunin' there kickin' the Pope an' that . . . ah mean, he's your boy's boss noo."

"Ah suppose ah'll need tae haun' ma rickety in?"

"Ach, they widnae ask ye tae dae that," Hughie said, shaking his head. "Ye wid be allowed tae keep it as a MOMENTO."

"Ah've been wonderin' where ah went wrang, Hughie," Andra said thoughtfully. "Ah should never hiv let him go tae see The Ten Commandments."

"Moses wisnae a Catholic priest," Hughie said.

"But it could've put the notion o' religion intae his heid," Andra pointed out, "ye can get easily swayed, Hughie. Look at Wullie

McSorley. Went tae see the Desert Song an' the last they heard o' him wis that he wis in Morocco wi' the French Foreign Legion. Pictures can sway ye, Hughie."

There was silence for a moment. Hughie was thinking deeply. Suddenly he made his mind up. Turning to Andra, he said: "Ah'll no' say a word, Andra."

Andra grasped him by the shoulders. "Ye . . . ye mean . . .?"

"Aye, ah'll no' let oan tae the boys. We've been chinas a long time, Andra. This terrible tragedy has nuthin' tae dae wi' you. It wisnae your fault." If Andra had been wearing his bunnet, he would have thrown it in the air. Delight shone in his face. "Ah Hughie . . . ye're a wee gem," he cried in relief . . . "a real pal."

Hughie was glad to see the smile back on Andra's face even if he did feel that he was betraying his cronies.

"Here," he said, handing Andra a ticket, "yer ticket for the match . . . only you an' me wull know," he gave Andra a knowing wink.

Andra shuffled embarrassingly.

"Whit's up? Hughie inquired.

"Hughie," Andra began, "noo that this is oot . . . ah . . . er . . . ah'm as well make a clean breast o' things wi' ye."

"Ye mean that there's MAIR?" Hughie said, wondering what was coming next.

"Aye, somethin' ah should have telt ye a long time ago," Andra replied, searching for words.

"Don't tell me YOU'RE a bloody priest?" Hughie was shocked at the thought.

"Naw, naw it's Annie . . ."

"She's a NUN?"

"Don't be bloody stupid," Andra snapped. "She's no' so easily swayed. She saw the Sound o' Music six times . . . naw, it's no' that."

"Well, for God's sake, whit is it?" Hughie pleaded.

"She . . . she . . . she's . . . er . . . wan o' them," Andra said with shame.

Hughie was dumbfounded. "Annie's . . . a . . . LESBIAN?"

"Aw, Hughie . . . sometimes ah think your heid zips up the back," Andra chided. "Naw . . . she's a PAPE . . . A CATHOLIC."

He never thought he would have to confess this.

There was a long pause.

"You must've known that a' the time," Hughie gasped at last.

"Of course ah bloody knew," Andra cried. "Ah've had tae live wi' it a' these years, hiven't ah? Tryin' tae keep it fae you an' the boys a' these years hisnae been easy Hughie."

"An' ye never let on" Hughie murmured.

"How could ah? Ye know whit the conversation's like doon at McDougall's."

Hughie knew only too well.

Suddenly his heart went out to his old friend. The torture, the turmoil he must have gone through. It didn't bear thinking about.

"Aw, ah'm sorry for ye. Andra," he said, "everything's tumblin' roon aboot ye . . . everythin' ye've ever lived for."

Hughie's comforting words were welcomed by a grateful Andra.

"It's no that Annie's been a bad wife, Hughie," Andra went on. "It wis her that kept the HP payment's goin' oan a' this stuff. Never wance did ah ever catch her sayin' her prayers . . . except when ah wis late comin' in wi' the buroo money. She even kept the Pope under the bed."

"Holy chambers, eh?" Hughie laughed. His quip made Andra smile.

"Well, Hughie . . . whit dae ye say aboot this other matter?"

"Ye can rely oan me, Andra," Hughie said, slapping Andra's shoulder, "Even this latest catastrophic news makes nae difference. Ah'll say nuthin'."

Andra sighed with relief. "Thanks Hughie," he beamed,

"Here, hiv another."

Andra topped up the glasses.

Peter lay on top of his bed cradling his head in his cupped hands. He could hear Andra and Hughie talking and laughing in the other room. Peace between them had obviously been restored. The conflict between him and his father was inevitable, he knew that. Perhaps there could be peace with them, too.

He would try once more. Andra was topping up Hughie's glass when Peter entered the room. "Is there one for me too?" he asked. Andra turned sharply. "YOU!" he exclaimed, not just at the audacity of his son daring to enter the room but to be asking for a drink as well. "C'mon dad, we shouldn't be quarrelling" Peter said. "What do you say?" Andra hesitated and then shrugged poured a glassful for his son. "Here," he said, without looking at him. Hughie beamed. "Aye, that's the wey it should be between a faither an' son," he said wisely.

"When dae ye get yer orders Peter?"

"He'll be gettin' his marchin' orders if he keeps up wi' this," Andra snarled.

Peter ignored the remark. "Ah'll become a deacon first, Hughie," Peter said.

"There, whit did ah tell ye," Andra interrupted, "he's gettin' a joab in a lighthoose."

"Ah said a DEACON, no' a beacon," Peter laughed, adding: "although ye might be near the truth . . . ah'll be showing the light."

For a moment Andra had thought that Peter might have had second thoughts and had dismissed the idea of taking the cloth . . . and giving him a showing up. But that last remark made him bite his lips in anger.

"Ye mean you're still goin' ahead with this mad scheme?" he grunted.

"Of course ah am," Peter declared. "Dad, ah'm a CATHOLIC," he emphasised the word, "ah've been confirmed."

"Aye, you're a confirmed bloody nutcase," Andra snapped back.

Peter threw his arms up in despair. "Ah'm tryin' to get through to you, dad. Don't you understand yet?" Peter shook his head.

"Aw, ah understaun' a'right," Andra said, shaking with anger. "Ah'm jist thankful that Hughie has consented tae say nuthin' aboot your flight fae the faith." Hughie puffed his chest out proudly. "That's right," he said.

"Am ah supposed to be grateful?" Peter asked. Andra stretched and pointed his finger half-an-inch from his son's nose. "Aye, you be grateful that ah'm no' slingin' ye right oot oan yer ear."

"Oh, aye, that would solve everything, wouldn't it," Peter said angrily. "When ye canny express yourself you turn to violence . . . typical!"

Andra flushed angrily. "Here you mind who ye're talkin' tae. Ah'm yer faither an' don't you forget it."

Hughie stood silent during this confrontation. He did not want to get involved in a family squabble, although he was down heavily on Andra's side. Peter, turning his coat, was bringing nothing but shame on Andra, McDougall's greatest stalwart, and HIS friend.

Andra's last remark bit deeply into Peter.

"FAITHER", his face flushed, "when were you ever a faither tae me? All ah can ever remember aboot you is cursin' and fitba' and booze. That's been your whole life. When did you ever take me . . . er . . . fishin' for instance?" Peter fought to control his emotions.

Andra's mouth fell open. He stood stunned. "FISHIN'?" he said incredulously.

"Aye, fishin' . . . or a walk in the country," Peter said.

Andra could not believe his ears. "A WALK IN THE COUNTRY?" Andra turned to Hughie with disbelief on his face.

"Aw, Hughie, this yin's away wi' the fairies. Fishin' . . . a country walk." He shook his head sadly.

"Ah like a wee walk in the country," Hughie said quietly.

"YOU walk in the country," Andra snapped, "it takes you a' yer time tae walk normally."

Hughie was hurt by Andra's sarcasm but decided to keep quiet for fear of really fuelling Andra's wrath.

Peter broke in quickly. "Ah have never let you down," he said. "You've never had any cause to worry about me . . . never."

"Well, ah've got bloody good cause noo," Andra retorted. "Ye've turned yer back oan every principle ah staun' for."

Peter flushed angrily. "AH have principles. What about ma principles?"

"You are jist doin' this tae get at ME!" Andra bawled.

"Oh, don't flatter yourself," Peter answered, keeping his shaking voice under control.

Andra shook his head. "Whit kinda bloody boy are you? Fishin', walks in the country . . . whit the hell's a' that aboot? Whit kinda boy . . ."

He did not get finishing the sentence. "Ah am YOUR son," Peter snapped.

"Ye're nae son o' mine," Andra came back. Peter turned on his heel. "In that case ah'll not stay where ah'm not wanted." Peter grabbed his coat and slammed the door as he made a quick exit.

There was a pause. Hughie became agitated. He wished he had been elsewhere during this clash of father and son.

"Stoap him Andra," he said nervously.

Andra shook his head. "Ach let him go," he murmured. Hughie could detect a sadness in his friend's voice.

"He's a good boy, Andra," Hughie said with concern, "ye shouldnae fight like that wi' him."

Andra turned on his friend. "It's nane o' your concern." he snapped.

"Ah'm yer freen, Andra," Hughie said quietly. Andra sighed. "Ah know, Hughie, ah know."

Andra poured another couple of drinks and the two men sat. There was a long silence. Andra was in deep thought. Last week everything in life was rolling along normally. Now everything was gangin up on him. How life could change so quickly!

"Never get mairried, Hughie," he sighed, "weans can be a curse."

"They don't always turn oot the wey ye want, that's true enough," Hughie said with authority. Andra nodded.

"Ye know Andra," Hughie went on, "ah nearly got mairried masel' wance."

Andra's eyebrows shot up. Hughie? Married?

"Is that so?" he said with surprise.

Hughie nodded. "Remember the time ah got that part-time joab at the convent when they were daen some renovations?" Hughie asked.

Andra nodded. "Ah mind it fine ," he said. "Nut only was ah shocked at you workin' in a convent . . . ah was stunned that ye were workin' at a'."

Hughie ignored the remark.

"Well," he went on, "there was this wee nun who used tae come oot noo an' again wi' a cuppa tea for me. An' ye know somethin' . . . ah fell in love wi' her." Andra stifled his laughter. "A NUN!" he exclaimed. "Naw, that would never work Hughie, nuns are wedded tae the church."

"Ah would hiv lived in sin wi' her," Hughie said dreamingly, "she was a wee beauty. Ah remember wance oor haun's touched as she gave me ma tea. Well, Andra, ma stomach turned an' leapt for joy. Oor eyes met an' ah jist couldnae find words tae say anythin'. But ah jist knew that ah had tae say somethin'. So ah cleared ma throat . . ."

"Whit did ye say, Hughie?" Andra said curiously. Hughie sighed. "Ah said . . . ah said . . . "Ur you a Catholic?" Andra threw his hands up. "Aw, ah despair for you, Hughie," he said.

Hughie came back down to earth. "Well," he said, "when she said she was that was it . . . ah mean, ye must get yer priorities right." He shook his head sadly. Andra nodded in agreement. "Aye, priorities," he said thinking deeply.

Hughie cleared his throat.

"Talkin' aboot priorities, Andra, ah hope ye don't mind me pokin' ma nose intae your business but ah couldnae help noticin' that Good King Billy isnae oan the wa'. Where is he?". Andra, embarrassed, ran his finger under his collar. Nodding towards the bedroom, he said: "He's in there . . . under the bed".

Hughie thought that one over. "Ah thought you jist said he was under the bed." he laughed. "Aye, well . . . er it was an emergency," Andra replied playing things down.

"Whit's he doin' there?" Hughie asked perplexed.

"Whit dae ye think he's doin," Andra snapped, "mendin' the bloody bed springs? He's mindin' his ain business, that's whit he's doin'." He wished Hughie would shut up.

"Ah don't think he'll like lyin' under the bed Andra," Hughie said.

"He's lyin' low, Hughie, lyin' low," Andra said, pouring another drink and hoping to steer the conversation into safer water.

Hughie sipped his drink. "Well," he said, "ah don't think it's very reverant," he said, concern in his voice, "Ah mean he's royalty, in't he?"

"Whit's that got tae dae wi' it?" Andra asked.

"Well, ye don't stick royalty under the bed even in an emergency," Hughie said. "Whit if ye had the Queen visitin' ye an' an emergency arose-"

"Ah really canny see the Queen poppin' up tae see me. No' in Brigton, Hughie . . . Bearsden maybe, but definitely no' Brigton." Andra was sure of his facts.

"But suppose she did," Hughie went on. "Say somebody came tae the door . . . somebody she didnae want tae see. Ye widnae tell her tae hide under the bed, would ye?"

"WHO would come tae MA door that Her Majesty widnae want tae see? Andra inquired.

"Well, whit aboot that big wumman fae Uganda for instance,"

"Whit big wumman fae Uganda?" Andra asked, wondering about Hughie's train of thought. "Big IDA Amin . . . her," Hughie said.

Andra shook his head in despair. "HE is a MAN, Hughie," he said contemptuously, "his name is IDI . . . IDI, Hughie, it's short for Idiot."

Hughie shrugged. "Well, him then."

"Ah don't know whit the hell you're talkin' aboot," Andra said, "but ye're right enough, Hughie, there's a loat in whit ye're sayin' . . . or no' sayin'. Billy is in an irreverent abode an it's time he came oot fae it." Andra hurried into the bedroom.

"Ye might hiv tae restore him," Hughie called after him.

Andra entered with his picture of King Billy and held it at arms length. Staring in awe at the precious painting he said:

"Ye're right, Hughie. The gloss has come aff him. Ah'll rub him doon wi' some whisky efter."

"Whit does that dae?" Hughie inquired, interestedly.

"Gies him a glow, Hughie, gies him a glow." Andra placed the picture on the wall, stepped back and genuflected in reverence.

Annie turned into the street. Her message bag was light as always but there was enough, always just enough. She hoped there had been no trouble at home. Andra would persist in trying to talk Peter out of his vocation, that was sure. She just hoped that things hadn't got out of hand. She pushed the door open just in time to meet Hughie leaving.

"Hello, Annie, ah'm jist leavin' . . . see ye at McDougall's Andra."

"Aye, McDougall's," Andra mumbled. Annie rested her bag on the table and quickly glanced around the room.

"Where's Peter?" she asked.

Andra didn't answer. "Where is he?" Annie snapped. "He's away," Andra said almost inaudibly. "AWAY WHERE?" her voice rose. "Tae Cathie's, ah suppose," Andra said without looking at his wife.

Whit have you been sayin' tae him?" Annie demanded. Andra shrugged. "Ah didnae ask him tae leave if that's what ye mean."

"Naw, but ye said somethin' tae him, didn't ye?"

"We had a wee chat", Andra said, flopping on to the chair and picking up his paper.

"And he's away?" Annie said coldly.

"Aye."

Annie turned on her heel and strode towards the door. "Well, ah'm goin' ower there an' if you've said anythin' tae drive that boy oot the hoose . . . you an' me are finished."

Andra leapt to his feet. This was the last thing he wanted. Annie was just angry enough to mean what she said. "Look Annie," he started . . . he stopped in his tracks.

Peter had entered. "Ah came back for ma books," he said without looking at his father.

"Aye, an' ye're stayin' back," Annie said going to her son's side, "isn't he Andra . . . isn't he?". This was an order and not a request. Just one wrong word and both his wife and son would depart from the house and Andra knew it.

"Aye . . . er . . . well, of coorse. Ah . . . er . . . didnae mean for ye tae go away in the huff, Peter." Andra said it almost apologetically, adding, "ye've got yer mither's temper."

"Aye, an' you're gonny see mair o' it fae noo oan," Annie snapped. Andra ignored his wife's anger. Silence was the better part of valour, he reckoned. Peter turned and walked towards his bedroom. "I'll . . . er . . . just go into the room an' study a while."

"You dae that, son," Annie said, ushering him out. "Ah've got tae get this hoose cleaned up . . . it's in a right mess . . . in mair ways than wan," she threw Andra a chilling look. "Ah suppose you'll be goin' tae the match the night?"

"Aye, well, . . . er . . . it's the replay," Andra found himself almost apologising again.

"Yer fitba' comes first in everthin', doesn't it? Annie said scornfully. "It disnae matter tae you that yer future son-in-law is comin' up here tonight wi' his parents. Ye're jist no' interested in anythin' or anybody but yersel'." Andra winced. Clarence, the very name made him cringe. The thought, too, of his parents calling filled him with trepidation. They probably talked with "bools in their mooth' he thought. What's a citizen of Newton Mearns wanting with a girl from Bridgeton anyway? Definitely suspicious, Andra thought. There was the undoubted celebration at McDougall's when their heroes would be toasted and glorified. He couldn't miss THAT. Besides if HE didn't show up it was a safe bet that his pals would be sending Annie a wreath in the morning. What else could keep him away?

Annie was still talking. "An' ah want tae see you sober," she was saying. "Ah don't want a showin' up . . . ye hear me?"

"Listen," Andra said, "if we win — ah mean WHEN we win — ah will be celebratin' in McDougall's as ah'll be expected tae be. Ah am no' that interested in meetin' whit's-his-name's folks." Then, as an afterthought, added: "Besides, ah wull probably no' be able to understaun' them."

"Whit dae ye mean by that?" Annie snapped.

"Well, they're foreigners, aren't they? Ah mean AH only know a few Arabic words . . . like shufti' an' that," Andra said.

"Whit dae ye mean SHUFTI an' that. They're as Scottish as you or me."

Andra shook his head vigorously. "Naw, Naw," he said, "THEY are a different breed. Ah mean YOU are gonny look silly when ye dish oot their tea. They don't eat ham ye know. You will hiv tae gie them their ain kind o' food if ye don't want tae antagonise them."

"An' whit kinda food is that?" Annie asked crossing her arms.

"Camel meat," Andra said with conviction, "whit they eat in the desert. An' where are ye gonny get that, eh? Big Erchie doon at the butcher's wull think ye're aff yer heid when ye go in an' ask him for a hauf-a-pun o' camel meat." Andra was pleased with himself. Annie threw up her arms in despair. "Whit are ye haverin' aboot?" she demanded.

"Listen," Andra said, "AH KNOW . . . you wull also hiv tae get a lumpy loaf."

"A lumpy loaf?"

Andra nodded. "Aye, they eat unlevelled breid. Boy, are you gonny hiv a red face!"

"You'll hiv a red face in a minute," Annie murmured. Andra was in full stride now and pressed on. "An' dae ye know how tae make lemon tea?"

Annie's eyebrows rose. "Lemon tea?"

"Aye, lemon tea. That's whit they bloody well drink. They don't drink ordinary tea 'cos it's made in India. They hate the Indians ye know . . . especially that yin Geronimo."

Annie thought for a moment, trying to find the connection. "Geronimo?" she asked quizzically.

"HE was a prophet of doom." Andra said with full knowledge.

"Dae ye no' mean Jeremiah?"

"Aye, . . . er . . . him as well," Andra said. "Anywey they get hauf-a-pun' o' lemons an' stick them in a teapot an' bile it up. It's foul, ah'm tellin' ye. It's no' bad in gin though."

Annie wondered why she was standing and listening to this rubbish. She turned and filled a kettle, saying: 'Ye're talkin' through a hole in yer heid."

61

"Hey, you watch it! Andra said, pointing a threatening finger, "You're getting brave in yer auld age. Ye might hiv Peter oan yer side but he hisnae got the twelve apostles wi' him." Annie turned. "AH don't need the twelve apostles tae deal wi' YOU," she said, her voice rising. "Things are gonny chinge around here — you mark ma words."

Andra ignored his wife's fighting spirit. "Well," he said, "ah am no' givin' in without a fight. It's bad enough Peter turnin' his coat. But Jean's no' only chingin' her religion . . . she is chingin' her race. Nut only wull she no' be a Scotswumman . . . she'll no' even be a Proddie."

"Whit dae ye mean?"

Andra shook his head. Did his wife not even know what he was saying? "She'll be a Jewess, won't she? Whit kinda bluenose am ah gonny be wi' a Jewess for a daughter an' a priest for a son?" He cradled his head in his hands and groaned slightly.

Annie responded immediately. "You jist keep yer nose oot o' it . . . blue or otherwise. THEY are goin' their ain weys and that's final."

Andra looked up angrily. "Nut as faur as ah am concerned," he bawled. "Ah don't like a' this inter-breedin'. Ye can cancel yer account at Goldbergs for a start. Jews don't hiv holy pictures that's another thing."

"An' neither dae YOUR lot," Annie replied, "unless ye think Oor Wullie up there is a holy picture." She nodded towards the wall. "Dae YOU look oan that as a holy picture?"

"Of course ah dae," Andra said with reverence. Annie pressed her point. "Dae you kneel doon sometimes an' say yer prayers in front o' it?"

Andra shuffled slightly embarrassed. "Ah hiv a wee blether noo an' again."

"Ye staun' there an' talk tae a hoarse.?"

"Ah do NUT talk tae the hoarse," Andra bellowed, "ah talk tae HIM. Whit aboot you an' yer chapel anywey? YOU kneel doon an' talk tae pictures."

"Rubbish," Annie retorted, "ah'm no' talkin' tae the picture. The picture only reminds me WHO ah am talkin' tae. It keeps yer mind fae wanderin'."

"Ah think this whole bloody family's mind's wanderin'," Andra said sadly.

Annie had Andra in a corner and she was not about to let him go. For years her husband had decried her religious beliefs. Now, she felt, she could get some of her own back. She went on: "Besides, it's pictures o' saints AH kneel tae. HE is nut a saint. That's another thing . . . how come he's no been made a saint?"

Andra shrugged. "Ach, he's probably got his ain reasons. Ye canny be a saint an' be mixed up in the fitba' scene."

"Whit aboot Saint Mirren?" Annie said smugly, referring to the Paisley football team.

"Huh," Andra sneered, "ye canny call that fitba'. You ur jist tryin' tae twist ma words."

'Y're twisted enough," Annie answered.

"Youse nut only hiv pictures," Andra ventured, "youse hiv statues as well. Ye're lucky ah don't bring in a bloody big statue o' Good King William — oan his hoarse."

"You jist try an' you, Oor Wullie an' the hoarse will be ridin' intae the sunset.

Andra strode towards the bedroom. The conversation was ended and, deep down, he wanted to quit while the going was good. Turning at the door, he snapped: "Ah'm goin' for a kip before the match. And HE is nut to be referred tae as OOR WULLIE. He is SAINT BILLY tae you," Andra vanished into the room, banging the door after him.

"Aye," Annie said to herself, "Saint Billy . . . the Kid!"

CHAPTER THREE

BURNS' NIGHT

Andra had arisen in plenty of time to deck himself out in his team's colours and leave happily for the big match. He had already put Clarence's parents right out of his mind despite Annie's sharp reminder about the visitors. There were more important matters at hand. The complete annihilation of Celtic filled his mind. What relish! He turned the corner and saw the bus already waiting outside McDougall's. His chariot to Heaven! Andra was a happy man.

Hughie was waiting for him at the bar. He could tell to the second when Andra would walk in and had a pint of export and "wee goldie" sitting on the bar to save time. Andra slapped Hughie on the back heartily. "Good on ye, China," he said, swallowing the whisky in a single gulp.

"Ye're aboot five seconds late," Hughie said laughing.

"Aye, Annie was givin' me ma instructions," Andra said, sipping his pint.

Hughie was surprised. "Annie givin' YOU instructions?"

Andra nodded. "Aye, this is the night that that big eejit's folk are comin' up."

"Aw, ye mean Clarence? Hughie said.

Andra spluttered in his beer. "Don't EVER say that word, Hughie . . . NEVER, d'ye understaun'? Ah get vulture pimples every time ah hear it."

"Ye mean GOOSE pimples, Andra"

"Naw, vulture pimples . . . they're bigger than goose pimples." Then Andra quietly asked: "Ye . . . er . . . hivnae said anythin' . . . tae the boys, ah mean?"

Hughie was hurt at the very suggestion. "Aw, Andra . . ." Andra was sorry he had even mentioned it. "Aye . . . er . . . sorry, Hughie . . . sorry!"

The bus had been found in Dundee with a painting of Desperate Dan astride a horse painted on it.

"Full o' comics," Andra commented. Hughie ordered another round while Andra scrambled in his pockets. He thanked Hughie, a friend indeed. "Ah'm jist a bit shoart, Hughie," he said apologetically, "but don't you worry ah'll make this up tae ye."

And the Pope will buy a season ticket for Ibrox, Hughie thought.

"Wait till ah get intae the Masons," Andra said with a glint, "then ah'll get somewhere, you mark ma words. Ah've already got Bowly McGeachie workin' on it . . . he's got a' the contacts, Bowly has."

Being the practical man that he was, Hughie remarked: "If Bowly McGeachie's got a' the contacts, how is it that he's always skint? Ah've never seen him dip intae his pocket yet."

"Don't you kid yersel', Hughie," Andra argued. "Bowly is a shrewd wee bloke. He's no' short of a bob or two. He gets his suits fae the best stall at the barras. Nae cheap stuff for him . . . although he DOES hiv tae get the troosers a bit longer than the jaicket tae compensate. If anybody can get me intae the masons, he can. Ah'll bet ma King Billy paintin' oan it."

There was no point in trying to reason with Andra, Hughie decided. He had his own thoughts on Bowly McGeachie.

"Maybe yer future son-in-law's faither has a better chance in gettin' ye intae the Masons," Hughie pointed out. "Doactors hiv a loat o' contacts."

Andra's eyes lit up. "Ye could be right, Hughie," he said, thinking that the night to come might not be wasted after all. "Aye, ye jist might hiv hit the nail oan the heid," Andra's mind was suddenly far away.

He was brought back to reality with the persistant hooting of the bus's horn. It was time to go. Andra and Hughie downed their drinks and joined in the happy chorus of their fellow fans. The singing reached a crescendo as the rolling bus speeded off with Andra's voice out-bawling everybody elses.

Annie, duster in hand, patted the chair cushion and stood back surveying her work approvingly. A crisp new table cloth draped the kitchen table and a vase of chrysanthemums splendidly graced the centre. The linoleum shone like marble. Annie was houseproud and, despite having to count the pennies, always kept her home spick and span. This effort was merely a little extra because of the circumstances. She still yearned for a house with a bathroom and had applied to the city corporation. She had reinforced her application with a novena to Saint Jude, the patron of lost causes. One day her prayers would be answered, she was sure of that. Her only worry was that Andra would arrive home in a fit state. If his team won, he would undoubtedly be celebrating. If they lost, he would be commiserating. One situation was as bad as the other.

She had carefully planned everything for this evening with Clarence's parents.

Salmon sandwiches were sure to be neutral she had decided and she had stretched her purse to purchase a bottle of sherry . . . which now sat for all to see on top of the highly polished sideboard. Annie was satisfied.

Jean finished tidying up the other rooms and entered mopping her brow.

"Whit dae ye think?" Annie asked proudly.

"The room's just lovely, mum," Jean said, squeezing her mother's shoulders.

"Ah widnae let ye doon, hen," Annie said with affection.

"You've NEVER let me down, mum," Jean replied, giving Annie another affectionate squeeze. "I just hope everything goes off all right."

"Yer faither's been well warned," Annie said sternly, "jist as long as he disnae bring that yin Bowly McGeachie in wi' him."

The thought of Bowly McGeachie being in the same room with Clarence's parents sent a shudder of horror through Jean's body. "Oh, he wouldn't mum, would he? Bowly McGeachie's just a wee con man!"

"Aye, well yer faither's up tae somethin' wi' him, ah can tell," Annie said, furrowing her eyebrows.

"Clarence's dad is such a gentleman," Jean said.

"He'll be the first wan yer faither's met," Annie replied with a titter.

The sound of car doors slamming sent Jean hurrying to the window. "Oh, mum, they're here," she called in panic.

Annie took it in her stride. She hurried to the wall mirror, preened herself and smoothed her gaily-coloured apron.

Others had gone to their windows, peering curiously into the street. It was not an every day occurence for a Rolls Royce to enter the street . . . never mind pull up and park. The last time was when Conk Kennedy, the close-mouth bookie, had collapsed running away from the new beat policeman. He died almost immediately and his shadowy bosses had given him the proper send-off for a man of his station.

Now another Rolls had brought a bit of class to the grey street. Who could have died this time? The question was asked by peering, inquiring eyes.

The man who stepped from the gleaming car stood tall in a dark-blue serge suit, cut in Savile Row perfection. The lady who followed had just stepped out of Vanity Fair. Her blue-silver-fox fur glinted expensively. The man looked up at the number on the closemouth, then taking the elegant lady's arm, guided her in gentlemanly fashion into the building. They vanished into the dark aperture and left curtains to fall back into place . . . and bewilderment.

Jean was already at the door while Annie gave herself one more patting of the hair at the mirror. She turned as Jean entered with Doctor and Mrs Burns. "This is doctor and Mrs Burns, mum," she said a little nervously. Annie stepped forward smiling and with outstretched hand. "I hope we're not too late," Mrs Burns said in the poshest accent Annie had ever heard. More Kelvinside than Newton Mearns, she thought. They shook hands. "Er . . . nae, c'min . . . c'min," Annie said, being as polite as possible. The tall doctor shook hands and smiled. "The traffic is very busy," he said. "Oh, ah know whit like it is," Annie lied, adding, "It's very nice to meet youse. Jean is always talking about youse."

"All good, I hope, Mrs Burns laughed.

Annie ushered her guests towards the settee.

"It'll be the match comin' out," Jean offered. The couple sat down and surveyed the Thomson abode. "Is Mr Thomson at the match? the doctor inquired.

"Oh, yes . . . but he shouldn't be long." Nodding towards the sideboard, Annie, from the side of her mouth, murmured — "Jean, the sherry."

Jean quickly filled four glasses, Mrs Burns sipped slowly, grimaced slightly and said: "I was just saying to Hector that you would have to have good wind climbing all those stairs every day!"

Annie nodded. "You get used to it," she said. "I'm up an' doon a' day . . . goin' tae the midden an' that."

Jean felt slightly hot under the collar and interrupted.

"I wonder what's happened to dad?" she said with some concern.

"It IS possible that my husband has stopped at McDougall's on his wey hame," Annie said, topping up her guests drink.

"McDougall's?" Doctor Burns inquired.

"Er . . . yes," Annie said with a slight, nervous cough. "It's . . . er . . . where he and his friends get together an' hiv a quiet talk about the gemme. They discuss the science of it . . . a kind of post-mortem oan the players' tactics an' that."

Doctor Burns nodded knowingly. There was an embarrassing silence broken finally by Mrs Burns who asked: "Are the buildings around here condemned?"

"Oh, aye," Annie replied, "they're condemned everywhere. We are hoping to move intae a multi-storey block. The bathroom would make such a difference. Youse wull hiv a bathroom of coorse?"

"Two, ectually," Mrs Burns said sipping her drink, adding, "It IS really needed in the morning — what with Clarence dashing off to college and Hector rushing for the surgery. It would be absolutely pandemonium if we didn't have two.

"Aye, ah see whit ye mean," Annie agreed.

"What does your husband do, Mrs Thomson?" the doctor looked genuinely interested.

"Andra, oh, he's what you call a sign writer," Annie said.

"That's interesting," Mrs Burns said with approval.

"Aye, he signs on the dole every Monday," Annie added, looking suspiciously at her empty sherry glass.

The Burns' laughed loudly. Annie and Jean joined in. The ice was broken. Jean refilled the glasses.

"He should be back fae the fitba' very soon noo," Annie said, rising and quickly glancing out of the window.

"Football is such a rough game," Mrs Burns said. "What about the old rugger, eh?"

"Nothing could stoap him goin' tae his precious fitba'," Annie said, shaking her head.

"Hector is a keen rugger player," Mrs Burns went on.

"Oh, RUGGER," Annie blurted, "ah thought ye said . . ." she did not get the chance to finish the sentence. Jean quickly interrupted: "More sherry everyone?" She poured without waiting for a reply. Doctor Burns nodded towards the wall: "I see you have a picture of King William there." It was a statement, not a question.

"Er . . . yes . . . er. Andra is a hoarse lover," Annie said, "he studies them every day as a matter of fact."

The Burns' glanced at each other but said nothing. "I like what you have done to your flat," Mrs Burns commented, changing the subject. "It's amazing what can be done with such small rooms. We have to have a cleaner in every day, our rooms are so huge."

"The only cleaner ah've got is a scrubber," Annie giggled. Mrs Burns laughed: "You have a great sense of humour, Mrs Thomson."

"Call me Annie," Annie replied, "an' ye would hiv tae hiv a sense of humour in this hoose or ye would go daft. In fact sometimes ah think Andra IS daft."

Andra and Hughie staggered into the street leaving a silent McDougall's behind them. "Bloody eejits," Andra moaned . . . "haddies," Hughie nodded. It was the wee man who first noticed the shining Rolls sitting at the closemouth. Gawking children were peering inside the windows while others attempted to remove the hub caps. "Look at that," Hughie said in awe as they came alongside. "Here ah thought you said the Queen wid never visit ye?"

Andra grunted, "Whoever belongs tae that big motor isnae up in ma hoose, ah can tell ye that. It's probably the Lord Provost canvassin' or the coalman doin' his rounds."

"It might be Clarence's faither," Hughie recalled, "is he no' supposed tae be comin' up the night?" Andra slapped his forehead, almost missing, "Gees ah forgot aboot that. Here, you better skeedaddle. This is faimily business, Hughie,"

"Ah understaun," Hughie said turning away. "Don't let him bamboozle ye noo," he added. Andra swayed as he entered the close and, holding the wall, climbed the stairs very carefully. He arrived at the door puffing slightly, took a deep breath and straightened his blue and white tile hat, flicked a speck of dust from his rosette and fumbled for his keys.

Jean heard her father's attempts to place the key in the lock and hurried to the door. "Oh, it's dad," she said in mock surprise. Andra staggered as he followed her into the room. Annie's look was less than gracious. She hurried to her husband's side and with one deft movement removed the tile hat from his head. "Andra, this is Mrs Burns," she said icily, "How do," Andra murmured, offering his hand. "And this is Doctor Burns," Andra nodded and shook hands.

"How did your team do?" the doctor inquired.

"Eejits," Andra said, "we wis doin' great right up tae the final whistle." He shook his head sadly.

"Oh, what was the final score?"

69

"Seven nuthin'," Andra replied almost whispering the words. Jean began to unfasten his rosette and removed the scarf from her father's neck. "I'll put these away," she said, "and never mind dad, there's always next year."

"They'll be in the fourth division next year," Andra groaned. Then, noticing the small sherry glasses in his guests hands, bellowed: "SHERRY? In MA hoose . . . c'moan, hiv a decent drink." Andra produced a bottle of whisky from his pocket and topped up three large tumblers.

"Noo, get that doon ye," he said thrusting a glass into an open-mouthed Mrs Burns's hand. "It'll dae ye good . . . an yer wee dug as well," he added, fondly patting her fox fur. Hector Burns raised his glass saying, "I like a good Scotch."

"That's the stuff," Andra said, downing his own drink and quickly refilling.

Jean made excuses that she had some studying to do and retired to her room.

"Everybody in this hoose is bloody studyin'," Andra complained. "They're jist tryin' tae get on," Annie said, drawing her husband her best "dagger" look.

Mrs Burns sipped her drink, shuddered and clearing her throat said: "I was just saying to Mrs Thomson . . ."

"Annie," Annie corrected.

"Yes, er . . . Annie, that she must be in good condition to climb all those stairs,"

"They're steeper when ye've got a good jug in ye," Andra slurred. "Here, ye're looking awfu' warm missus. Wid ye no' like tae remove Dougal there?"

"It IS rather warm," Mrs Burns agreed.

Andra stepped forward, grabbed the fox fur and tossed it into the bedroom, slamming the door in case of escape.

"Ah'll bet the bloody mice in there get the fright o' their lives," he sniggered.

Annie looked on dumbfounded. Before she could reprimand her husband, Doctor Burns stood up and inquired: "Could you tell me where the smallest room is?

"Of course," Annie replied, "Andra . . . where's the torch?" Andra shrugged. "The bulb's done . . . ye'll jist hiv tae use matches."

70

"The toilet is on the stair, Doctor, ah'll show ye," Annie said, scrambling in the sideboard drawer for a box of matches.

"I have my lighter," Doctor Burns said smiling, "and do call me Hector."

Annie smiled. "This wey, Doc . . er . . . Hector."

The two left with the doctor testing his lighter. There was an uncomfortable silence in the room. Mrs Burns shifted uneasily on the couch. Andra was watching her closely, then leaning over her he whispered: "Has yer granny got a wart oan her bum?"

Her mouth fell open. "I beg your pardon?" Mrs Burns wondered if she had heard correctly.

Andra furrowed his brows. "YOU know whit ah mean."

"A wart? . . . on her bottom?"

"Oan her BUM . . . that's the proper jargon," Andra said irritably.

"Well . . . really," Mrs Burns sounded affronted.

"Ach, jist forget it . . . you're obviously no' wan of THEM," Andra said with disappointment. "I haven't an inkling what you are talking about," Mrs Burns went on.

"Look, whit ah mean is . . . hiv ye ever had yer grip? . . . you know," he winked, "the auld shake o' the haun'? Naw, ah suppose no' . . . THAT phrase wid be too coorse for wimmen. Youse probably say it with mair delicacy — like has yer granny got a PLOOK oan her bum . . . is that it?"

Mrs Burns relaxed. "I see," she said, "I think I see what you're getting at. I'm afraid my grandmother is quite unblemished."

Andra shook his head. "A pity," he said, but it was worth a try."

Annie and Doctor Burns entered. "My heaven's it's dark out there," said the doctor.

"It's worse withoot the torch," Andra commented. "Ah miss every time."

Annie felt her face flush and quickly changing the subject suggested to Mrs Burns that she take her a guided tour of the house.

"A good idea, Annie," was the response and the two women left leaving the men to get on with their business.

"Well, that was diplomatic enough," Doctor Burns said.

"Er . . . aye . . . ere, here let me fill yer gless," Andra said pouring a large one for both of them. The doctor raised his glass. "Bottoms up," he said.

"Speaking of bottoms," Andra said, "Has your granny got a wart oan her bum?".

"As a matter of fact she had," the doctor replied, "I removed it."

"Well, how aboot that, then," Andra yelled. They emptied their glasses and Andra qickly refilled them.

"Tell me," the doctor said, "does your uncle clean his balls with Brasso?"

Andra's whisky sprayed out in a jet stream. He spluttered and wiped his dribbling chin.

"WHIT?"

"Your uncle," the doctor said, "that's what they call the pawnbroker, right? His balls . . . the three brass balls which is the pawnbroker's sign. And Brasso for cleaning them . . . all right?"

Andra was dumbfounded and could only stand with his mouth open.

The doctor went on, "You were trying to find out if I am a Freemason."

"Well . . ." Andra began.

"You should get your signs right. As a matter of fact I am not one of that exclusive body."

Annie and Mrs Burns entered, crossed the room and vanished through the other door . . . "an' this is Peter's room," Annie was saying.

Andra nodded, "It's ma greatest ambition . . . tae be a Mason," he said. "Ah was nearly in them wance but the chap that was tae be ma sponsor met wi' an accident. He gave this bloke the auld shake o' the haun' an' the fella turned oot tae be a catholic Kung-Fu expert."

"So, that was it up in the air?" said the doctor.

"That was HIM up in the air. He's still in the hoaspital," Andra said, shaking his head.

Doctor Burns placed his half full glass on the table, "Look," he said, "I think it's about time we got down to business." Aye, ye're right," Andra agreed, "but ah can see a loat o' problems here?"

"What problems?"

"Well . . . er . . . there's the religious thing an' that," Andra said, pulling himself up to his full height.

"I don't see any problem there," the doctor said.

"Ah but there is. An mean WE arra people, aren't we? Ye've got

Catholics an' Protestants . . . but they're Christians. Right enough the Papes think that they are the chosen people. That's whit causes animosity, int it? Ah mean, YOU think that YOU are the chosen people . . . that's bigotry, y'see? Bias! Ah mean it's a well known fact that WE are the chosen people. Ah know we got skelped at Ibrox the night but that disnae count. Ah jist could nut staun' bigotry in ma ain family circle."

Andra poured himself another large one.

Doctor Burns sat down and sipped his drink. "I see," he said. "I er . . . believe your son is going into the priesthood?"

Andra shrugged it off. "Aye, but he is temporarily insane. He's been brainwashed by Charleston Heston."

Doctor Burns nodded. "Heston can be a persuasive fellow." Andra went on. "Ah mean YOUR race has pinched everythin' it's got . . . ye've even taken OOR names. Whit's yer Christian . . . ah mean . . . yer . . . er . . . first name?"

"Hector."

Andra slapped his thigh. "Ah-ha . . . there ye are, y'see. Whoever heard o' a Jew wi' a name like Hector? Even yer second name, Burns, pinched fae OOR national poet. Okay, ye might feel ye've got the right tae use it 'cos his first name's Rabbie . . . but it's still stealin' . . . knockin'. Even that general ye've got . . . him wi' the Long John eye patch . . . Moshe Dyan . . . that's a good Glesga name."

"Dyan is a good Jewish name," the doctor corrected.

"Ah . . . but Moshe's no'. Ah used tae play moshie when ah was a wee boy . . . three holes in the grun' an' ye chucked pennies intae them. See whit ah mean?"

Loud laughter could be heard coming from the bedroom.

"Ah wonder whit THEY'RE laughin' at?" Andra said, puzzled. "Maybe they've found something in common," Doctor Burns mused. Andra shook his head. "Naw, that's impossible. We're a race apart. You're a' brithers . . . a kind o' britherhood, in fact. That's how ye don't join the masons . . . ye've got yer ain private clan. Ah don't know if youse shake hauns or rub noses. Ye've probably got yer ain signs."

Doctor Burns shrugged. "I've no idea and I'm not interested. I'm kept pretty busy enough. A doctor's life isn't an easy one, you know. Often I get calls in the middle of the night."

"Me tae," Andra replied, "but ah can never find the bloody torch."

Andra had forgotten that his guest was a doctor and an idea just occurred to him "Aye . . . er . . . being a doactor ye . . . er . . . must know a few dodges for gettin' panel lines, eh?"

"Not as many as you, I'll bet," the doctor smiled.

"Ah am chronically sick and gettin' worse a' the time," Andra said grimacing and holding his back. "Even the doactor says ah'm sickenin'."

"We all have our crosses to bear," the doctor said.

"Well, you lot should know aboot that," Andra said sarcastically.

"You know," the doctor went on, deciding on a new tack, "I think you're pretty smart. YOU summed up everything perfectly. You are dead right to object to this marriage. You've made me see sense."

"Ah hiv?"

"Mabel, that's my wife," the doctor continued, "thought that Clarence and Jean should be given a chance. But I can see that you are right. It would never work . . . a hard studying Jewish boy from the other side of the tracks . . . and a girl from . . . er . . . Bridgeton. The whole idea is ludicrous."

Andra felt his face flush. "Are you sayin' that our Jean's no good enough for your Clarence?"

"How could she be? They have completely different backgrounds . . . not to mention the religion aspect."

"Whit dae ye mean?" Andra snapped.

"Do I have to spell it out to you," Doctor Burns said. "Look around you. Clarence is at teachers' training college because he WANTS to go. Jean is only there because she is trying to escape from her environment. It's understandable."

"Oor Jean disnae hiv tae escape fae anythin'. In fact she likes ironin' . . . she disnae want tae escape fae that. Whit a bloody stupid thing tae say . . . Jean's tryin' tae escape fae her ironin'!"

Doctor Burns stifled a smile. "No," he said, "Jean is not for Clarence. He can drop her like a hot matzo."

"Zatso, matzo?" Andra said, his voice rising angrily. "Well ah think your Clarence is doin' bloody well for hisel' gettin' oor Jean. She could hiv had anybody . . . the midgie man is daft oan her. But if it's Clarence she wants, it's bloody Clarence she'll get an' you an' bloody Mabel can keep yer big noses oot o' it."

"I'm not sure," the doctor said, shaking his head.

"Bloody cheek," Andra said, pouring himself another drink.

"It's the way things are," the doctor said. Andra gulped his drink and poured another, even larger one. Pointing his finger defiantly at the doctor he went on. "Ah widnae like tae be wan o' your patients. Ah'll bet when somebody walks intae your surgery wearin' dungarees ye gie him a jab oan the erse wi' a ten-feet long needle."

"All I'm saying is that it just wouldn't work," the doctor said, ignoring the sarcasm."

"Of coorse it would bloody work," Andra hollered, "EVERYTHING works."

"You don't," the doctor replied with a slight smile.

"Aye . . . er . . . it's ma back," Andra said, holding his back and pulling a painful expression.

"Okay," the doctor said, "let's have a look at this famous back."

"Ah'm no' peyin' ye," Andra said quickly.

"Roll up your shirt," the doctor said advancing on him. Andra rolled up his shirt protesting all the time. The doctor gave him a few hefty jabs on the back. Andra screamed in mock pain, toppling over the back of the couch and landing, panting on top. He lay writhing and groaning . . . "Ah'm dyin' . . . ye've killed me," he complained.

"You'll have to put your back into something," the doctor said.

"Ah am nut wearin' wan o' they corsets," Andra said sharply.

"I meant something like a hard day's work," the doctor replied. "There's nothin wrong with your back that exercise at a job wouldn't cure."

Andra did not like the direction this conversation was going. This man was suggesting that he should go out to work. He was obviously an imbecile or a super optimist. If he told Annie that his bad back was a good back all his years of agony play acting would have been for nothing.

"As a matter of fact," the doctor said, "I happen to be a director in one or two companies. "I'm sure I could get you fixed up in a suitable job."

These were words that Andra had never wanted to hear. He had perfected the art of malingering. He had never once been offered a job from firms the employment exchange had sent him to. He once borrowed auld Horace McGroarty's wheelchair presenting himself at the building site for an interview. This jibbering doctor could be a threat to everything he stood and worked for.

75

"It would never work," Andra said.

"You mean that you would never work," said the doctor. He had Andra summed up perfectly. He was rarely wrong in his diagnosis.

The doctor produced his wallet and taking a business card began to write. "This will assure you of a job," he said, "just take it down to the McLean Iron Foundry and you'll be fixed up."

Andra exploded — "IRON FOUNDRY? Ye want tae kill me? Ah don't know anythin' aboot iron . . . except that it goes intae Scotland's other national drink. Naw, naw . . . ma back would never allow it."

The doctor shrugged. "We'll see," he said.

The conversation was interrupted by Annie and Mrs Burns entering the room the "tour" being over. "An' that's the coal bunker," Annie was saying, adding, "Are youse men finished wi' yer discussions?"

"Are we?" Doctor Burns asked, giving Andra a serious stare.

"Ah am still against this weddin'," Andra said emphatically.

"Are you sure?" Doctor Burns produced the business card and stroked his cheek with it.

"Oan the other hand," Andra said quickly "there might be . . . er . . . room tae negotiate."

"There will be NAE negotiations," Annie said sternly. "Jean and Clarence are gettin' married an' that's final . . . ye understaun', Andra?"

"I'm glad that's settled," Mrs Burns said, smiling. "No bias in this house."

"BIAS?" Andra threw his arms in the air, "nut-at-all. We hiv oor ain beliefs an' that's it. Look at the wa', there. That's Billy, the GREAT Billy. He is the cleverest man that ever lived. He is the wan that started the Orange Walk. We would walk for miles behind him. Aye, he was a shrewd man.

"Obviously, HE isn't walking, is he?" Doctor Burns said with a wry smile.

"THAT is a faithful hoarse," Andra said ignoring the doctor's remark, "a clever cuddy, that. They say it's Red Rum's great grandfaither. They should have called the hoarse Orange Rum, eh?" Andra laughed.

Mrs Burns sat on the couch, crossed her legs and smoothed her dress. "Well, I'm glad that everything is settled," she said, "Now, how about four weeks on Monday, Andra?"

"Well, if Hector an' Annie don't mind," said Andra laughingly, "where wull ah meet ye?"

"I mean the wedding," Mrs Burns said, blushing.

"Hey, wait a minute!" Andra exclaimed. "It's no' a bloody shotgun affair. Has that dirty swine?" . . . He did not finish. Doctor Burns moved quickly.

"No . . . no . . ." he said placating Andra. "It's just that Mabel and I are going to Australia for a year and we would like to see Clarence settled before we go. We understand that Jean has no objections."

"And where is this weddin' tae be?" Andra asked fearing the worst.

"In the synagogue, of course," the doctor said in a tone that meant there would be no arguments. Andra turned quickly to Annie. "See, that's it started. Ah've got Saint Peter for a son an' Golda Meir for a daughter."

"Shut yer face," Annie snapped.

"You shut YOUR face," Andra retorted. "Bloody Julie Andrews."

"Look," the doctor said, "our house is going to be empty while we're away. The young couple can have the use of it. It's practical, isn't it?".

"Because YOU'RE goin' doon under that disnae mean these two should be bulldosed intae gettin' doon under," Andra hollered.

Mrs Burns turned to Annie. "We WOULD like to be at the wedding. This trip to Australia has taken ages to arrange and we've been planning it for years. Hector would like to see his family before we get much older. They're natives of Australia." Andra shook his head in disbelief. "Geeze," he groaned, "they're everywhere. Even the bloody kangaroos are Jews."

"ANDRA," Annie chided. Andra shrugged.

"Well, can we take it that that's everything settled?" Mrs Burns asked, giving Andra a long, stare. It was Annie who answered. "Ye can take it frae me that everythin's settled. If that's whit they want, that's it." She too, gave Andra a long menacing stare.

"Good," Mrs Burns said smiling, "I'm so glad!"

"Right," Annie said, going to the table where the food lay under a protecting table cloth. "Noo, how aboot somethin' tae eat?"

"We proamise no' take gie youse ham," Andra said. Mrs Burns jumped to her feet, smacked her hands together and laughed. "Right, get the scoosh oot then an' lets hiv a good bevvy."

Andra's mouth dropped open at this sudden degeneration. Where

77

had the posh accent gone. The finesse? Mrs Burns read his mind. "Aye, Andra," she said, "ah came fae the Gorbals and ah never forget it. Hector an' me had the same problem mair than twenty years ago. Ah'm no' Jewish either but ah studied the faith and then ah got magired."

"It was lucky you was gettin' hitched tae a doactor . . . he would soon cure ye o' that. There was a loat o' that . . . er . . . magired goin' aboot then." He shook his head. "Imagine youse bein' in the same boat, eh? Is that whit youse two were laughin' at oot there?"

"Aye," Mrs Burns laughed. "Ah told Annie all about it an' we decided to keep up the pretence."

Laughter resounded around the room. Andra gave Mrs Burns a hearty slap on the back and soon the festivities were in full swing, Jean having joined in happily with Clarence arriving later. Jean hugged her father. "Ye're no' married yet," Andra said with a slight bitterness in his voice. Things had gone too fast for him. The "engagement" had suddenly steam rollered into a wedding. His approaches to Doctor Burns about entering the Masonic order got him nowhere. But maybe the sly doctor was being secretive. Wasn't that the name of the game in that esteemed brotherhood? Drawing Doctor Burns aside, Andra whispered quietly, "That . . . er . . . phrase aboot yer uncle an' his Brassoed balls . . . is that . . . er . . . wan o' the true . . . er . . . signals?"

Doctor Burns smiled. "It's as authentic as your granny's wart," he said.

Andra walked away thinking deeply. He took a large swig from the whisky bottle and shuddered as the golden liquid hit his stomach.

Looking at Clarence, dancing in the middle of the floor, he shuddered again. If only he could keep all of this a secret . . . but he knew that the news would eventually get around. The nosy neighbours, the aproned mafia, would have already been making inquiries into the purpose of the Rolls Royce at the closemouth.

He would think up some excuse to divert inquisitive minds. The Rolls could belong to anybody . . . his rich uncle from Texas . . . the Grand Master of the Exhalted Prairies Ludge.

More than once during the evening's celebrations he had shown his disapproval of the impending marriage but, at the first hint of dissent, out would come that obnoxious business card. It was blackmail pure and simple and he did not like it one bit. He wondered if Doctor Burns was a director of some other, more appropriate, company. A

78

brewery, for instance! It had not been a good day for Andra Thomson. Fights with Annie, this 'Burns Night' confrontation . . . not forgetting the Hampden farce. It was just an off day for the boys, he decided. Probably a big day in the Catholic Calendar . . . Saint Vincent de Ball, or something. He had heard of him.

In the meantime he was as well 'getting a bevvy' with the rest of them. Tomorrow was another day. Tomorrow he would study the book of masonic secret signs Bowly McGeachie had given him. There are always clouds before the sun shines. Things could only get better . . . he hoped!

CHAPTER FOUR

BOWLY McGEACHIE'S PLAN

Bowly McGeachie tapped his foot impatiently and dragged on his Woodbine. He had arranged to meet Wullie O'Reilly under the umbrella at Bridgeton Cross at one o'clock. The news of the Thomson wedding had already reached him and he could see a way of cashing in on Andra's misfortune. Bowly was an expert in the art of grasping opportunity. He had lost no time contacting Andra with a proposition . . . one that Andra had jumped at. Everything now depended on Wullie O'Reilly, not the brightest of sparks but, under Bowly's direction would suffice. Hence the arranged meeting under one of Glasgow's most famous landmarks — 'The Brigton Croass Umberrella'. The Umbrella was the hub of all Bridgeton's main roads. Like the spokes of a wheel, they fanned out — London Road, to Celtic Park, Dalmarnock Road, to the Power Station, Main Street, to Shawfield where the greyhounds raced and James Street — to the south side and Ibrox Park.

Bowly glanced up at the clock on top of the monument. It showed twenty past one. Bowly lit another Woodbine from the half-inch remaining on his cigarette. He must brief Wullie once more before introducing him to Andra. Wullie could easily jeopardise his plan. Andra COULD get angry . . . and Bowly had seen Andra angry. He could take no chances. Relieved, he saw Wullie hurrying across the road coming from the direction of London Road. Wullie was panting and had obviously been hurrying to keep his appointment.

"Whit kept you?" Bowly snapped.

"Ah'm sorry, Bowly, it was an emergency joab at Dalbeth," Wullie gasped. Bowly shuddered at the name of the East End Catholic cemetry.

"Ah'd proamised tae hiv this auld priest's gravestone finished an' in place by this moarnin' but the joab took longer than ah planned."

"Well, ye're here noo," Bowly said. "C'moan, we'll hiv a drink." Wullie's eyes lit up and the two men crossed to the pub in Dalmarnock Road. Bowly ordered two large whiskies at the bar, indicating to Wullie to sit at a corner table. Settled down, they got into a huddle.

"Noo," Bowly said, "ye know whit ye've tae say? Ye must let Andra

Thomson think that ye're a Freemason . . . he's Masons daft."

Wullie was not sure that he could 'carry it off'. "But ah don't know anythin' aboot the Freemasons," he protested, "AH'M A CATHOLIC."

Bowly reeled. "For God's sake don't, but DON'T, mention that in front o' Andra. He'll murder us baith. As faur as HE'S concerned YOU are a Freemason an' ye run a wee baun'. Ah mean, ye WANT the work, don't ye? Yer boys want new gear for the Hibernian Walk, right?"

Wullie nodded. His band was still wearing cast-offs from the previous band who were now pensioners. "Aye, we could dae wi' the work, right enough," he agreed.

"Well, look . . . HE thinks you're gonny get him intae the Freemasons," Bowly reiterated, "jist play it cool." Wullie was not sure about all this. "Ah'm jist a stonemason," he pleaded. "A' ah make is gravestones doon at the graveyard." "Wullie, if you don't watch yer tongue we'll baith be needin' wan o' your gravestones," Bowly said, shaking his head. He was beginning to wonder if this was a good idea. "Please, nut only for God's sake but for MA sake, don't mess this up Wullie," he said pleadingly.

"Ah'll dae ma best," Wullie said without conviction. Bowly ordered two more drinks and the men went over the strategy again . . . and again.

Bowly could do no more. He bought a half bottle of Bell's and they left the pub. Wullie was now in a happier mood and the cold air outside made him happier still.

They crossed the road and turned into the Main Street and headed towards Andra's house. Bowly would get a percentage of Wullie's fee although he wondered where Andra would get the money to pay up. But he knew Annie. She was much more thrifty and would never allow her daughter's wedding day to be marred by anything. Annie would already have her budget well planned. He was sure of that.

Bowly and Wullie stopped in at McDougall's for a booster before continuing their journey. Suitably fortified and rehearsed they left.

Two weeks had passed since the "Burns Night" and Annie had been getting affairs organised for the forthcoming wedding. It had not been without its frustrations. Andra had kept up a tirade of objections. The jollity of the celebrations had vanished with the hangover. He knew that Annie would walk out if he continued with the diatribe . . . not forgetting Doctor Burns' little blackmail card. He was cornered. He had talked things over with Hughie Broon who, being the good wee friend that he was, had said nothing to his pub cronies. He could maybe just get away with it. Jean would vanish to Newton Mearns and out of sight. He would never mention THAT if the subject ever came up in conversation. He would say that she had moved to the Calton, near the "Barras" to a wee "single-end". There would be no obvious change in Jean's appearance to give things away. She wouldn't be wearing a sari or anything like that. Andra was glad that Clarence was not an Indian. It could have been worse, he reckoned. Clarence could have been a Catholic Indian. You must count small blessings, he supposed.

Peter's position was entirely different. Andra shuddered when he thought of it. His son WOULD stick out a mile. The clerical collar was a badge proclaiming to all the world the calling of the wearer. He wondered if Peter would consider wearing a six-inch wide collar?

It would look more like a surgical appliance then. That was worth considering. He decided that Peter would not. He would just have to buy him a scarf. Yes, that was the answer . . . a scarf . . . a Rangers blue and white team muffler. It could be that Peter might not pass his examinations. It was more than a week now since his son had gone through them and there was still no word whether he had scraped through or not. He put his trouble to the back of his mind. Bowly McGeachie would be arriving at any minute. Andra had been faithfully studying the little book Bowly had graciously given him. It contained all the secret signs he would have to learn once installed in the lodge. Andra reckoned that the lodge must be "teemin" with cash . . . all those big businessmen contributing to its coffers. It was ridiculous that their little guide book was hand written, smudged with mis-spellings galore. It should certainly have been printed . . . in gold letters, Andra thought. Still, there was probably a good reason, he shrugged.

The job might have been given to a Catholic printer and that would have been treacherous. Yes, they knew what they were doing! Andra glanced at the mantleshelf clock. Bowly was late. Probably caught up in some big business deal, Andra decided. He relaxed in the couch and brushed up on his Masonic homework. Annie and Jean were preparing to go out and putting a final touch to their appearance.

"Noo, ye're sure ye're gettin' this baun' organised?" Annie asked with a hint of threat. Andra put the book down. "Ah telt ye tae leave everythin' tae me. Ah should be clinchin' the deal anytime noo."

82

"Whit dae ye mean 'clinchin' the deal'?" Annie asked suspiciously.

"Ah am killin' two burds wi' wan stone," Andra replied smugly.

Jean was worried.

"You've left everything to the last minute dad," she said with consternation. "What if things go wrong? What if the band doesn't show up? Who can have a wedding without a band? Oh, I'll have a red face."

"Aye, an' so will yer faither," Annie snapped. "Don't you worry, Jean, everythin' will go accordin' tae plan. Yer weddin' day will nut be marred, ah proamise ye that. An' as for YOU," she said, turning to Andra, "whit dae ye mean 'killin' two birds wi' wan stone'?"

"Ma greatest wish is aboot tae be fulfilled," Andra said, with a broad smile. "Aboot tae come tae fruition."

"And WHIT is that?" Annie said, folding her arms and staring at him fixedly.

"Nut only is the bloke who has the baun' a musician. He jist happens tae be a high heid yin in the Masons. Bowly McGeachie has arranged this momentous meetin'. They wull be here in a minute. Durin' the conversation ah wull make sure that he gets the message. Bowly gave me this wee book wi' a' the pert ... er ... percival signs."

"Aye, well jist as long as ye get that baun'. An' as for Bowly McGeachie, he would say anythin' for a free drink. If ah was you, ah would nut believe a word o' that book."

Annie was biased, Andra thought.

"C'mon, mum, we'll have to be going," Jean tugged at her mother's arm.

"That is Bowly's gospel," Andra said in Bowly's defence. Rising, he added, "Ah am jist goin' doon tae the cludgey before he comes. It's a' that bloody black puddin'. Where are youse goin', anyway?"

"Ower tae Cathie's," Annie said.

"Whit for?" Andra said with a grimace. Andra did not particularly like his wife's sister.

"Something old, something new, dad," Jean said with an impish smile.

"Somethin' borrowed, somethin' blue," Annie finished the old adage.

"Well, see if ye can get back that hauf pun' o' tea she "borrowed" last week. An' the only thing blue ye'll find ower there is her man, wee

83

bachley Boabby ... she's too mean tae light the fire. He'll be sittin' freezin'." Andra made a hurried exit.

Annie turned to Jean. "Ach, yer faither goes too faur at times," she said. "Ye get fed up wi' this nonsense."

"Well, mum, you just put your foot down," Jean said. Annie nodded. "Ye're right, Jean. For a start it's aboot time that AH had a friendly face lookin' doon at ME. An' ah know jist how tae rectify things."

Taking Andra's picture from the wall, she reversed it and slipped the picture of the Pontiff inside. Then she replaced the picture on the wall with the Pope looking down in the position of blessing. Annie stood back and surveyed her handiwork. She smiled a satisfied smile. She never did like the picture of Andra, dressed in his supporter's togs and with that "stupid grin" on his face.

Annie crossed her arms and defiantly took in the scene. She smiled. "There you are, your Holiness ... don't let Oor Wullie there annoy ye."

Jean laughed. "When dad sees that he'll have a heart attack," she said, giggling.

"Yer faither will jist hiv tae accept it," Annie said dryly. "If this man, who is allegedly high up in the Masonic order, sees that picture, it might jeopardise dad's chances of being admitted," Jean pointed out.

"Huh," Annie said scornfully," dae ye really think a high paid yin fae the Masons is comin' up HERE?

"Jean, am a Catholic an' ah've got nuthin' against the Masons. They no doubt dae a loat o' charity works ... and anythin' that's done for charity can only be a good thing. But dae YOU really think that they're gonny admit yer faither intae their ranks, eh? They'll no' even take him in the Orange Ludge. the only place yer faither's no' barred fae is McDougall's."

They were interrupted by a sharp rap on the door. "I'll get it," Jean said. Annie gave the Pope a naughty wink and stuck out her tongue at his companion on the wall. She turned as Jean entered with Bowly and Wullie.

"It's Bowly McGeachie, mum," she said with disdain.

"Aye, well ye better come in," Annie said with scorn in her voice. "Andra's expectin' ye. He'll be back in a minute — unless he's got the Sportin' Life wi' him."

"Nae hurry, Annie, nae hurry," Bowly said jovially . . . "This . . . er . . . is Wullie."

"You run a baun'?" Annie said pointedly. Wullie nodded eagerly. "Oh aye, missus, it's a great baun' a great baun'."

"It had better be," Annie said sharply.

"Hiv nae fears, Annie," Bowly said quickly, "Ah'm his agent . . . a position ah haud amongst ma other business activities. Ye maybe did nut perceive that ah am quite musical masel'."

"Ah know that ye're good at blawin' yer ain trumpet," Annie said with sarcasm.

"But Bowly's no' in the baun', Mrs Thomson," Wullie was emphatic. "He's no' on the trumpet."

"Oan the fiddle mair likely," Annie said contemptuously. Turning towards the door, she said: "We canny wait." Pointing to the couch she ordered: "You two sit there . . . an' don't you dare move till Andra gets up." Before leaving, Annie turned back and, taking the alarm clock from the mantleshelf, secreted it in the sideboard drawer. "Noo, you two stey put, hear me?" She did not wait for an answer and mother and daughter left albeit with their suspicions.

Bowly and Wullie sat twiddling their thumbs until they were sure the two women had gone.

"Awful suspicious wumman, that!" Wullie remarked.

"It's no' her ye've got tae worry aboot," Bowly said seriously. "Jist remember . . .".

Before he could finish his sentence, Andra came into the room grumbling: "Annie's black puddin' is gettin' worse." His countenance changed immediately he got sight of Wullie.

"This . . . er . . . is Wullie, Andra," Bowly said rising, "he might be able tae dae you a favour . . . TWO favours, eh Wullie?"

"Er . . . aye, that's right," Wullie said, stammering slightly.

Wullie tapped his head twice, stuck his tongue out from the side of his mouth and rubbed his stomach in a clockwork direction. Andra was elated and replied by sticking his thumbs in his ears and waving his fingers.

"Away an' kiss a goat's erse," he said to Wullie. Wullie's mouth dropped. "Eh?" he stuttered.

"AH hiv kissed a goat's erse," Andra said with a broad smile.

"Aye . . . er . . . well ah hope ye rinse yer mooth oot when ye eat yer chips," Wullie replied, glancing at Bowly and shrugging his shoulders. Andra quickly took the book and quickly flicked through the pages. Speaking slowly and directly, he said: "Ma hammer has a claw." Wullie took up the tenor saying: "Ma cat has got four." Andra, continuing to read from the book, went on: "Lillies droop in the spring."

"She should get stronger elastic," Wullie replied. Andra frantically flicked through the pages trying to find the meaning of Wullie's reply. Bowly, seeing what was happening, intervened: "That's too advanced for you Andra . . . understaun?" Bowly gave a knowing wink.

"Ah get it, ah get it," Andra replied with a wink. Turning to Wullie, he said, "Ah . . . er . . . didnae catch yer name?"

"Wullie O'Reilly," Wullie said.

"O'REILLY!" Andra blurted, "O'REILLY!"

Bowly quickly stepped in. "Aye . . . er . . . a direct descendant o' the Great Chief O'Reilly who led the Orange charge at the Boyne in 1690." Bowly mopped his brow.

"Oh aye . . . er . . . of coorse," Andra mumbled, his eyebrows furrowing.

"You are very fortunate to acquire Wullie's baun' for yer daughter's nuptials," Bowly said with pride. "It jist so happened that he had tae cancel a bookin' when a heard ye were lookin' for a baun'."

"Is that a fact?" Andra said, "Where is yer bookin'?"

Before Wullie could reply, Bowly intervened. "At Balmoral," he said, breathing on his fingernails. Andra's brows shot up. He was suddenly impressed. "Bamoral, eh?" If Wullie's band had an engagement at the Royal Family's Scottish estate, it should be good enough for his Jean.

He looked at Wullie respectfully. Wullie put a finger up his nose and patted his head three times. In reply, Andra tapped his elbows and winked knowingly. He HAD heard somewhere that the Duke of Edinburgh was a member of the Grand Masonic Lodge. This would undoubtedly be one of the main reasons that Wullie's band was given the engagement. It made sense. Turning to Wullie, Andra said: "Is it true what they say aboot Dixie?" Wullie looked at Bowly and tapped the side of his head. He was not referring to a masonic sign. "Does the sun really shine a' the time," he replied to Andra.

"Do the sweet magnolias blossom at everybody's door?" Andra said, tapping his heel and doing a half turn with one arm in the air.

Bowly, getting caught up in this musical excursion, could contain himself no longer. Falling on one knee, he sang with gusto . . . "Is it true what they say about Swanee . ." Andra grabbed him by the scruff of the neck and hauled him to his feet.

"We can hiv the Jolson medley efter," he snapped, "let's get doon tae business."

Turning to Wullie he said: "Noo, apart fae playin' at the reception, ah would desire that your baun' play at the close when Jean is leavin' for the weddin' ceremony."

Wullie nodded. "Nae bother," he said. "It'll no' be the first time we've played in the street."

"Whit?"

"Ootside Buckingham Palace," Bowly said, slapping Wullie on the back . . . "Command performance."

Andra was impressed. "Buckingham Palace, eh?"

Wullie nodded. "We hiv oor regular bookins'," he said proudly. "For instance, we play every week for the Union of Catholic Mothers."

"WHIT?"Andra bellowed.

"Ye've heard o' THEM, Andra?" Bowly said, cooling what could be a dangerous situation. "The Union of Carbolic Mothers . . . a bunch o' wimmen cleaners who haud a wee dance every month . . . ye must've heard o' them, Andra?"

"Ma hearin' must be goin' wonky," Andra said, poking his little finger into his ear.

There was a moment's silence. Wullie wondered what all the fuss was about.

"Wance we even played at a special presentation for Jesuits," Wullie said with pride.

Before Andra could say a word, Bowly quickly intervened: "Aye, what a wumman that was. Ye must know her, Andra . . . she used tae run that wee sweetie shoap in Gallygate . . . Jess Ewits." Bowly stared angrily at Wullie. "It was a retirement do for the auld sowel."

"Ah canny say ah know her," Andra said shaking his head and once more poking a finger in his ear.

"Hiv nae fears, Andra," Bowly went on, "Wullie here has the contract for a' the BIG places. Tell him, Wullie, tell Andra aboot yer latest bookin'."

87

Wullie just stared blankly. "Y'know, Wullie, yer bookin' for the . . . you know . . . the Masonic . . . y'know?"

Wullie suddenly remembered his briefing. "Aw, THAT bookin'," he cried. "Ach we jist take that kinda bookin' in oor stride." Andra's ears pricked up at the word "Masonic". "Whit bookin' is that, Wullie . . . the Masonic . . ."

"Aye . . . it's . . . er . . . the Masonic Legs . . . a very important hostelry."

"ARMS, Wullie — Masonic Arms," Bowly said with frustration. "He gets a bit mixed up, Andra. He's got that many bookin's oan his mind."

"Bowly, are you sure he's a' there?" Andra said, "are ye sure he's got a' his jorries?"

"Andra," Bowly said with a hurt expression, "how could ye doubt? HE is wan o' US. Ye know ah widnae gie ye a bum steer."

"As long as it's no' a bum baun'," Andra said, ashamed that he had doubted Bowly's word. Slapping his hands together, Andra cried, "RIGHT . . . let's hiv a drink tae celebrate."

Bowly and Wullie rubbed their hands in anticipation. Andra poured liberal amounts. They toasted and drank. Andra replenished the glasses.

"Whit dae ye call yer baun', Wullie?" he said, making conversation.

"The Hibernians," Wullie said with a proud nod if his head.

Andra spluttered.

"Aye . . . er . . . they play a loat for the Bernie Inns," Bowly said, grabbing the bottle and topping Andra's glass, "great restaurants, them."

"Ye had me worried, there," Andra said, still shaking slightly. "Dae ye ever get yer baun' tae play for yer granny?"

"Eh?" Wullie turned and looked pleadingly towards Bowly.

"You know . . . yer granny's birthday for instance," Andra winked.

"Ma granny's birthday?"

"Ma granny's two hundred years auld," Andra said thinking about the lodge he wished to join, "whit aboot yours?"

"My granny's jist a wean o' eighty-two," Wullie replied. Andra wondered where Lodge eighty-two might be located. "Eighty-two, eh?" he said. "Ah would like tae get together wi' your granny — if ye see whit ah mean." Wullie shrugged. "Please yersel'," he said, "she's in an auld folks home in the Gallygate." Old Folks Home, Andra thought. Brilliant! They have Lodges hidden everywhere.

"The wan in the Gallygate is jist for auld folk Andra . . . no' for the likes o' you," Bowly said knowing what Andra was thinking.

"Whit aboot HIM," Andra said pointing to Wullie. "Ye canny tell me that HE'S an auld man."

"Wullie has been gettin' treatment, Andra, he disnae look his age."

Andra stared at Bowly. "Whit did he get, a bloody heid transplant?"

Lodge eight-two in the Gallowgate. He would remember that.

"C'moan, let's hiv another drink," Andra said smacking his lips. He poured.

"We wull raise oor glesses tae the boys up there oan the wa'." Andra stood with his back to the pictures making sure that Wullie and Bowly were toasting with due reverence. Bowly raised his glass: "To Billy," he said.

"An' his hoarse," Andra added. Wullie raised his glass and with a quiet aside murmured — "Ah hope you are roastin' in Hell."

Andra choked on his drink. Had he heard correctly? Bowly quickly dampened the situation. "Aye, he will be, Wullie, he will be."

"Am ah hearin' right?" Andra bellowed.

"A' Wullie said was that he hoped Billy would be toastin' as well. Whit's up, Andra?"

Andra shuffled his feet. "Er . . . nuthin'," he mumbled. "For a minute ah thought . . . ach, never mind."

"Ye can be sure that he is toastin' us fae his heavenly abode," Bowly said.

"Dae ye think he sees us fae where he is?" Wullie asked.

"Of coorse he does," Andra replied, wondering how a man like Wullie could possibly doubt such a thing.

"He must hiv a bloody long periscope," Wullie said, sipping his drink.

"WHIT?" Andra screamed, poking his ear once again.

"Wullie says that he must hiv a bloody long telescope . . . tae look doon from his celestial throne," Bowly was quick to reply.

"Aw, ah see," Andra shook his head. His hearing was definitely deteriorating.

"Ah see ye've a picture of a real fine man up there, tae, Andra," Wullie said, raising his glass to Pope John.

Andra did not turn round. He was unaware that Pope John's picture now stared out from the wall in place of his own. Coyly, he said, "That's very kind o' ye Wullie. That is the very latest gear for wearing' at Ibrox. That picture was actually taken oan the terracin' . . . the crowd was booin' at the time."

"Ah'm no' surprised," Wullie replied. Bowly just gaped. He reckoned the picture was on Andra's wall for a purpose. He would say nothing.

"Note the position o' the haun's, Wullie," Andra said proudly. "Ye know whit that means, don't ye?"

"Somebody's gettin' blessed?" Wullie said innocently.

"Somebody's gettin' MESSED, Wullie . . . that is a karate posture," Andra said, wondering if Wullie's eyes were as bad as his own ears. "Ah can always remember the day that was taken, he said, his eyes gleaming as he recalled. "Ah am talkin' aboot HIM . . . Good Pope John," Wullie said, pointing to the picture.

Andra spun round. He gasped when he saw the Pope's picture on the wall. ANNIE — she did this. He flushed with anger and began to stammer an excuse.

"THAT is NO' the Pope. He jist looks like him. THAT is an auld mafia chief Annie got roon the barras. It's tae hide a crack oan the wa'."

"Ah think there's a crack oan your heid." Wullie said, "THAT is definitely Pope John . . . a finer man never lived." Bowly was hiding his head in his hands.

"Who's yer pal, Bowly?" Andra said gesturing towards Wullie.

Bowly sidled up to Andra and whispered in his ear.

"Calm yersel' Andra . . . it's jist a wee test."

Andra winked. Turning to Wullie, he said: "Ma granny has a wart oan her bum."

Wullie hiccupped. "If she's two hunner years auld, it's a wonder she's no' lumpy a' ower," he said.

Andra flicked through his book. "Fish hivnae got fingers," he said, mouth open and waiting for an answer.

"Saves them fae buyin' gloves, din't it?" Wullie said, now with the courage to replenish his own glass.

90

Andra did not understand the reply but pressed on: "Ma dug has got six legs," he said.

Wullie thought for a minute before replying. "In that case you should enter it at Shawfield," he said. Wullie sneezed and blew his nose. Andra flicked frantically through his book muttering . . . "nose blawin' . . . nose blawin' ah canny see it. Whit does it mean when he blaws his nose, Bowly?"

"It means he's got a bloody cauld, Andra . . . nuthin' sinister."

Andra was still not sure where Wullie's lodge might be located and was anxious to know. He recknoned that the old folks home in the Gallowgate was just thrown in to put him off the track. This was understandable as, no doubt, Wullie was sizing him up. They couldn't be too careful, he knew that. It would not be right to allow just any riff-raff into the ranks. He would ask Wullie quietly and in a round about fashion just where his lodge lodged. "Tell me Wullie, where . . . er . . . where dae ye dae yer thing . . . you know,"Andra asked quietly.

"It's no' a thing ah like tae talk aboot," Wullie said.

"Ah can understaun' that," Andra agreed.

"It's a gruesome subject tae some people," Wullie added.

"Aw, ah widnae describe it as gruesome," Andra said, "secretive maybe . . . no' gruesome."

"It's funny, though," Wullie went on, "Catholics don't seem tae mind. They're always at me tae make them wan."

"CATHOLICS?" Andra was shocked. But it stood to reason that they would give anything to infiltrate the hallowed Lodge.

"When did ye last make somebody wan?", Andra asked curiously.

"Jist earlier oan the day, that's whit kept me late."

Wullie was truly a dedicated man, Andra thought. "Was it a big businessman?" he asked. Wullie shook his head. "Naw, naw," he said, "a ninety-nine year auld priest." Andra stood stunned. "A ninety-nine year auld priest?" he mumbled, "Geez, whit a last minute convert. That's amazin'." Bowly had decided to say nothing. Andra filled the glasses. "Look, Wullie," he said, "ah'll lay ma cards oan the table. Could ye make ME wan?"

"There is nuthin' ah'd like better," Wullie said with a slur.

Andra was delighted. "Jist like that?" he said, snapping his fingers.

"Nae bother," Wullie said, "but it'll cost ye seventy quid."

Andra's face fell. "Ah didnae know it was as expensive as that," he muttered.

Wullie shrugged. "For you ah'll make it fifty . . . but nae angels."

"Whit dae ye mean, ANGELS? Whit hiv angels got tae dae wi' it?" Andra was perplexed.

"It means ye'll no' get yer wings right away," Bowly said, breaking his silence.

"Oh, ah see," Andra said, nodding.

Wullie shrugged. "It's up tae you," he said, "dae ye want a gravestone or no'?"

"Ye don't need tae get a bloody gravestone tae get in, dae ye?" Andra uttered in disbelief.

Wullie shook his head. "Naw, naw," he said, "it's up tae you. It'll be you that's gettin' buried."

"BURIED?" Andra's echo bounced around the room. "Who the hell wants tae get buried. Ah hiv heard o' initiatin' ceremonies but tae hell wi' that."

Wullie shrugged. Andra paused and thought for a moment. Perhaps he was being too hasty. Obviously the brethern would have to test his loyalty. The burial would no doubt be A SYMBOLIC GESTURE . . . perhaps the burying of the past. He turned to Wullie: "When dae they dig ye up again?"

"Aw, they don't dig ye up again," he said shaking his head.

"Look," Andra argued, "ah know it's a secret society . . . but it's no' that bloody secret that they bury ye' an' hide ye oot the road."

"If ye don't like the idea o' gettin' buried there's always the other way," Wullie said.

Andra's ears pricked up. He was claustrophobic. If there was a better way, he would take it. "Whit wey's that?" he asked.

"Get cremated," Wullie said coldly.

"CREMATED?"

"It's cleaner," Wullie said.

"Aye, an' bloody final," Andra said angrily, adding: "How could ah turn up for the bloody meetin's, eh? Ah can jist see the majestic brother staunin' up there an' sayin' . . . 'Ah would like for youse tae meet oor new member . . . that's him ower there in the ashtray."

Wullie looked over at Bowly. "Whit's he talkin' aboot?" he asked, puzzled.

"Ah am talkin' aboot the Freemasons," Andra snapped. The penny dropped. Wullie slapped his thigh: "Aw, ah thought ye were talkin' tae me in ma capacity as a stonemason . . . ma trade."

Steam came from Andra's ears. "Ye mean ah hiv wasted a' this time talkin' ma wey intae the bloody grave?"

"You jist leave everythin' tae Wullie," Bowly said, pacifying Andra. "Mark ma words."

"Ah'll mark yer face if anythin' goes wrang," Andra said angrily. "You jist make sure that him an' his baun' turn up at the closemooth tae play oor Jean intae the motor."

"We'll dae her proud, Andra," Wullie said beaming. "When ye hear ma baun', yer feet wull be tappin'."

"An' ah'll be there tae supervise things personally," Bowly said.

Andra nodded. When he and Bowly had been talking about the masons there had obviously been a big mistake. They had been talking at cross purposes. It was too bad but not the end of the world. Bowly pulled Andra aside. Whispering in his ear, he apologised. "There's been a grave mistake here, Andra," he started. "Grave is the right word," Andra said. Bowly went on, "It's Wullie's brother that's a Freemason. Even Wullie disnae know that. It was jist a wee mix-up, that's a'."

Andra was willing to give Bowly the benefit of the doubt.

"Here," he said, "hiv another drink before ye go. Nae hard feelin's." Andra poured the drinks. Putting his arm around Bowly's shoulders he said, "Y'know Bowly, ah've oaften thought it was a shame that folk called you Bowly jist because yer legs were bent . . . bent a good bit right enough. So, ah am goin' tae stoap callin' ye Bowly. How aboot that?"

"That's very good o' ye, Andra," Bowly said smiling.

"Forget it," Andra said, giving his shoulders a squeeze. "Fae noo oan ah'll call ye Bandy."

Bowly gulped his drink. "C'mon, he said to Wullie, "we'd better be goin'."

Andra ushered them towards the door. "Don't worry," he said. "Ah'll hiv a boattle in ma poacket at the weddin' an' we'll hiv a good few scooshes, eh?

He smacked his lips.

Wullie turned at the doorway. "Aye," he said, "but Andra . . . when ye pass the boattle tae me, jist make sure ye hivnae been kissin' any goats erses first."

93

The men laughed.

Bowly and Wullie left. At the foot of the stairs, Bowly pushed his crony against the wall. "Whit was the idea?" he snarled. "You could've got us baith hung up there." Wullie shrugged. "I canny tell a lie," he said, "jist like George Washington."

"YOU'RE mair like George Formby," Bowly snapped, "glaiket."

"Well, the main thing is we got the bookin' for the baun'," Wullie said, satisfied. Something of the encounter had been salvaged and Bowly was only too glad they had left the Thomson house in one piece. "C'mon," he said, "we'll hiv a snorter."

The two men walked into the street and headed for McDougall's.

Andra was disappointed. He lit a cigarette and filled a glass. Walking over to the picture of Pope John, he raised his glass. "You're probably delighted," he said. "Well, ah'll get ma ain back oan you."

Annie would probably expect the offending picture to be removed. No! Andra would leave the picture where it was. He'd been thinking about getting a new dartboard anyway. His only worry was that King Billy, who was hanging adjacently, might take offence. "I hope your Majesty wull bear wi' me for a wee while," he said apologetically. "This is jist a temporary measure until ah get organised. Before ah'm finished, that wull definitely but definitely be the holiest picture in Glesga. There wull be mair holes in it than the puttin' green at Rothesay."

If Annie said anything he could always blame it on woodworm. He thought he spotted a smile flitting over Pope John's face.

He chided King Billy for not coming to his aid in his hour of dire need. No doubt he was busy in more important matters.

CHAPTER FIVE

WEDDING DAY

The wedding day had come around very quickly. Andra's protestations had fallen on deaf ears. He had tried every ruse he could think of in an effort to get Jean to change her mind. Annie and Mabel Burns had become great confidantes, his wife even visiting the Burns' mansion in Newton Mearns. What a climb down, Andra thought. Mabel had even visited Annie still wearing "that stupid dug roon her neck." Peter had been very quiet and was still waiting patiently for news of his exams. No news is good news, Andra reckoned. It could be that his son had flunked and Andra could see Peter taking up the plumber's tool bag after all. That, at least, was some consolation. He sighed . . . a man defeated. He sat on the couch, lit a cigarette and sighed once more. He could hear Jean moving about in her room. She was humming happily. Clarence would probably be doing the same, he thought. Stupid idiot! He had seriously thought of boycotting the wedding. When he had finally conceded that nothing would stop the wedding, he got the idea of handling the reception arrangements himself. Unfortunately the Orange Hall was already booked for a bookie's wife's birthday party and the Bridgeton Public hall was being re-decorated. Annie had flung her arms up in horror when Andra had told her of his intentions. They would have the reception in the Windsor Restaurant at Bridgeton Cross, she had decided.

He would have to nip in the bud these meetings between Annie and Mabel, he thought. His wife was getting tarred with the Newton Mearns brush. And as for the guest list? It read like a who's who of folk Andra did not wish to attend. Cathy and her sponging man for a start. He had licked his pencil struck out eleven names suggesting they be replaced by the Rangers football team. He had even made inquiries at Ibrox but a polite letter arrived thanking him but, with regret, declining. The Grand Master of the Orange Lodge had, unfortunately other commitments and could not attend either. He wondered if Annie had invited the Archbishop of Glasgow? The "toffy" way she had been carrying on could not rule this out. Another few weeks with Mabel and Sable and she would have been inviting the Pope, he thought. Hughie had been invited and had been well warned by Annie to turn up in his best attire. She was not going to get a showing up by Andra, Hughie or anybody else on her daughter's wedding day.

Hughie was delighted at the thought of being invited and had already invaded "The Barras" for suitable gear. Andra had apologised to his McDougall's cronies who had not been invited to the wedding. They were just having a quiet affair, he told them . . . a quick trip to the Register Office and fish suppers at the groom's house near the barras. The boys understood. They were a good bunch. He only hoped that none of them would be hanging around Bridgeton Cross and see the wedding party troop into the Windsor. He had already inquired if the restaurant had a back door.

Andra dragged on his cigarette and shook his head sadly at his lot. Jean entered, still in her dressing gown. "Dad," she said.

"Whit?" Andra said without looking up.

"Are mum and Peter not back yet?" she asked anxiously. "Time's getting on."

"Aye, it is, int it?" Andra replied, "time's gettin' oan."

Jean sat on the arm of the couch and affectionately stroked her father's hair.

"C'mon dad, let's see a smile," she said. "This is all part of life. It happens in every family. The chicks must leave the nest."

"Ah've loast you an' ah've loast Peter," Andra said, shaking his head. The world was crushing him.

"You haven't lost me. You'll probably see more of me than you do now," Jean said reassuringly.

"Aye, the hoose wull be full o' gran' weans before long," Andra shuddered at the thought. "A' stickin' their long noses intae everythin'. Ah'm no' ready for that."

"I won't be a mum for a long time yet," Jean answered.

"Looking at Clarence, that disnae surprise me," Andra said sarcastically.

"There's nothing wrong with him," Jean laughed, "believe you me. He wants six sons . . . and he's going to have them."

"That'll no' surprise me either," Andra smirked, "You'll be pacin' the corridor ootside while he's in labour. Six sons, eh? You know whit he's doin', don't ye? He is buildin' up the bloody Israeli army . . . wi' MA gran'weans. Bloody ironical!"

"What is?"

"You're goin' away tae become a mother an' Peter's goin' away tae become a father," Andra shook his head.

"Och, don't be so silly. Peter will make a lovely priest. He's got a lovely countenance about him," Jean said.

Andra grimaced. "He should hiv a bloody straitjaicket aboot him. Ah'm surprised he can go tae this weddin' an' associate with atheists."

"Clarence's people are not atheists," Jean said in defence.

"Naw, but AH am," Andra snapped.

"Oh, you are not," Jean said in rebuttal.

Their conversation was interrupted by a knock on the door. "I'll get it," Jean said, hurrying to answer. Andra heard giggling and Jean entered accompanied by a well proportioned young lady of her own age. "Dad, this is Maureen my best maid," Jean said in introduction. Andra smiled and shook her warmly be the hand. "Aye," he said, "ah believe that you are at college wi' ma Jean?"

"That's right, Mr Thomson."

She WAS a big girl, Andra thought.

"Maureen, eh? That's Irish, int it?"

"My grandparents are from Cork," Maureen replied smiling. "That's why ye're a wee corker, eh?" Andra laughed. Jean decided to break up the conversation in case her father should get carried away.

"If ye like to go into the bedroom and get ready Maureen, I'll be in in a minute," she said steering her towards the door. Maureen turned and gave Andra a friendly wave before vanishing into the room. "I'll not be long," Jean called after her.

"Nice lookin' lassie that," Andra commented. "Too bad she's a Pape."

"Oh, Maureen's not a catholic, dad."

"Is that a fact?" Andra said, "Wi' a name like that, tae."

"You can't go by names," Jean said. "As a matter of fact Maureen's a Buddhist."

Andra was stunned. "Geez," he stammered, "you'd never know. She's no' even a bit baldy."

Andra was still thinking about that when Annie and Peter burst in. Annie leaned against the door, catching her breath. Then, catching Andra's eye, she pointed an accusing finger and hollered — "Ur YOU no' ready yet? C'mon, get crackin' . . . the caurs will be here soon."

Turning to Jean she gasped: "Has Maureen arrived yet?"

"She's in the room getting ready," Jean said.

"She's a Buddhist," Andra said.

"Never you mind whit she is. At least she's in there gettin' ready, that's mair than YOU'RE doin' . . . move it."

Turning to Jean once more she said apologetically: "Ah'm sorry ah was so long, Jean. Ah jist had tae go tae Mass oan yer weddin' day."

Jean kissed her mother's cheek "I understand, mum," she said quietly.

"Of course she does," Peter said. Andra looked on contemptuously.

"An' another thing, Jean," Annie went on, "ah've asked Father McGinty if he would come along tae the synagogue an' reception an' he said he'd be delighted. Ah hope ye don't mind."

"Of course not," Jean replied. "He's a lovely wee man."

Andra turned purple with rage. "Whit a weddin' this is goin' tae be, eh? Priests and rabbis. Hiv ye no' sent an invitation tae the bloody Ayatolah? Don't sit that bloody priest or rabbi next tae me, ah'm tellin' ye that."

"You'll be at the top table, dad. The cantor will be next to you," Jean said. "The cantor, eh? Andra said thoughtfully, "Ah thought he was deid. Ah don't mind that, ah like him . . . "If you knew Susie", an' a that."

Peter and Jean hid a smile.

"Well, c'mon, Jean, intae the room wi' ye. We hivnae a lot o' time." Annie ushered Jean towards the bedroom door. Turning, she bellowed at Andra — "An' as for YOU . . . YOU get in there an' get intae that hired outfit if ye know whit's good for ye." Andra grunted and Annie vanished, slamming the room door behind her.

Andra and Peter were left alone. Going over to the sideboard, Peter produced two glasses and poured a couple of large Scotches. Handing one to his father, he raised his glass. "Well, dad?"

"Well, whit?" Andra said sourly.

"This is the day you've dreaded, isn't it?" Peter said.

Andra did not reply. He sipped his drink and gave a long sigh.

"You should be pleased for Jean," Peter said. "She's got a nice lad there. Clarence will do well in the world. He's a hard worker."

"Don't gie me that crap. He was born wi' a silver cutlery set in his mooth," Andra said bitterly.

"So, good luck to him," Peter answered, refilling the glasses. Andra grunted.

"There's something else you're as well to know," Peter said pulling a letter from his pocket. "Ah got this today . . . ah've been accepted at the seminary."

Andra said nothing. He stood up and, gulping his drink down replenished his glass. This certainly was not his day. Turning to Peter, he gave his son a long, hard stare. "You hate everythin' ah staun' for, don't ye?" he said quietly.

Peter shook his head. "No, dad, ah don't."

"Ye hate the Rangers an' the Ludge."

Peter sat on the arm of the couch. "No, no, d'ye no' understand yet?" he said. "Look, there are good Orangemen and there are bad Orangemen an' there are good Rangers fans an' bad Rangers fans . . . people that neither wants tae know. Just like there are good Catholics and bad Catholics . . . and good and bad Celtic supporters.

It's that small minority that causes all the damage. They're like a cancer ye can't get rid of. They're the hangers-on. Just trouble makers and bigots. A good protestant is better than a bad Catholic."

Andra raised his eyes in surprise.

"You think there are BAD Catholics? Ah'm surprised at YOU sayin' that!"

"It's always been ma belief," Peter went on. "But you wouldn't know that. Ah mean, when did we ever sit down an' talk, really talk?"

"We used tae . . . when ye were a wee boy," Andra said quietly.

"But all you ever talked about was fitba' and . . ."

"That's whit every faither talks aboot tae his boy," Andra interrupted.

"Look, dad," Peter said, "It's no' every boy that's interested in fitba'. There are other things to talk about."

"Like, WHIT, for instance?"

"Well, there's religion . . . politics . . . work." Andra did not like that last word. Peter was still talking. "You've got a narrow mind, dad. You only see in one direction. Take religion for instance. What's YOUR church?"

Andra thought that one over before replying. "Ibrox is ma church," he said finally.

"See what ah mean," Peter said throwing his arms in the air. "Ibrox is a fitba' ground."

"Naw, naw . . . it's mair than that," Andra said quickly, "mair than that."

Imagine Peter thinking that Ibrox Park was JUST a football ground. Andra shook his head in disbelief.

"It's Rangers home ground," Peter argued, "they're a great team . . . it's a SPORT, dad . . . a SPORT. You shouldn't mix up a great sport wi' religion. God does not support Rangers . . . or Celtic . . . or Partick Thistle."

"He difinitely didnae support them at the cup final, that's for sure," Andra admitted sadly.

"God loves EVERYBODY, dad . . . he's got no favourites," Peter said with authority.

Andra shook his head vehemently: "Ye're wrang there, pal," he said. "How aboot a' they rich folk? they're loaded an' ah hivnae got tuppance. Ye canny tell me that's no favouritism."

"It's easier for a camel to go through the eye of a needle than a rich man to get into Heaven," Peter replied, quoting the scriptures.

"Well," Andra snarled, "there's no' many camels aroon' here . . . although, mind ye, wi' a' these Arabs an' Indians flockin' in . . ."

"See, there you go again," Peter said despairingly. "Don't forget it's the ones who suffer most who will reach the promised Kingdom, who will receive the brightest crown. Kings, all of them,"

"Bloody maharajahs, ye mean," Andra said with a sneer. "Naw there are those who get it an' those who don't. Ah wish he would show ME some favouritism an' drop a few bob ma wey . . . nae favourites, huh?"

"Money is the root of all evil," Peter said, "it corrupts. Greed is the greatest sin. Money talks, there was never a truer word."

"Well, ah must need a bloody hearin' aid," Andra grumbled.

"Money isn't everything," Peter went on. "It wipes away principles."

"Well, there's nuthin' will wipe away MA principles," Andra retorted. "Ah know whit ah'd dae if ah had plenty o' money."

"Aye, ah know as well," Peter said. "If somebody offered you a million pounds you would no doubt become a Rangers director, eh?"

"If somebody offered me a million quid ah'd even become a CELTIC director," Andra answered.

"See with ah mean," Peter pressed his argument. "Principles go by the wayside."

100

"Ach, it's a' pie-in-the-sky," Andra said with a shrug. "There's them an' us an' that's the way things are."

"You must live and let live, dad," Peter said. "You're mad at Jean marryin' a Jewish chap . . . a really nice bloke. What would you have said if she had fallen in love wi' a Chinaman or a Pakistani, or . . ."

Andra exploded. "A CHINAMAN? A PAKI?"

"It could easily have happened," Peter said.

"Ower ma bloody deid boady," Andra rapped. "You'll no' get ma Jean walkin' aboot wi' wan o' they safaris oan stinkin' o' curry. They should be sent back tae Gunga Din land anywey."

"Britain would collapse without them," Peter said in defence. "When you went to the hospital to get that phoney back of yours x-rayed was it no' an Indian doctor and nurse that attended to you?"

"Aye, an' ma back's still bloody sore," Andra complained.

"Your Scottish doctor doon the road didn't cure it either," Peter said, with smug satisfaction.

"Naw, but at least ah could understaun' whit he was bloody sayin'," Andra snapped. "He talked tae me in ma ain idiot. That Paki was jist a' teeth. A' he could talk tae me aboot was bloody cricket."

"Well, that's THEIR favourite sport. You talk about Rangers an' fitba' all the time."

"No' a' the time," Andra said, "jist maist o' the time. Besides THAT is a man's gemme. Naw, we're too tolerant, that's the trouble. Too many foreigners gettin' intae the country. Walk doon Sauchiehall Street noo an' it's like bein' in the bloody Punjab."

Andra shook his head. "We've even got Arabs buyin' good Scoattish stately homes."

"Ah thought you were against stately homes?" Peter said with a grin.

"Ah definitely am. But ye must ca' the line when the Red Shadow gallops in an' snaps them up. The only Red Shadow ah want tae see takin' over is the Brigton Croass Communist Party."

"Oh, you're a communist now?" Peter laughed. Andra nodded. "Ye must look after the interest o' the workin' man."

"That lets you out, then," Peter said grinning. "Now let's see . . . that makes you Red, Orange an' Blue . . . you should really join the Rainbow Party."

Andra did not appreciate his son's flippant remark.

101

"There's wan thing that ah'm no' . . . an' that's GREEN," he said. "You're jist mockin' me because o' ma principles."

Peter shook his head. "No, no," he said. "I'm all for folk having principles . . . it's when they try to force them down everybody elses throat that I'm against. You must bend a wee bit to the other bloke's point of view."

"No' if he's wrang," Andra argued.

"Who's to say that he's wrang and that you're right?" Peter argued. "Let's look at YOUR prnciples. You've been bending backwards to join the Masons. What's your principle motive, eh?"

Andra shuffled his feet. "It's the brotherhood, int it . . . the brotherhood."

"When were YOU ever interested in the brotherhood of man?" Peter said with contempt. "You're just like millions of others. Your motive in joining is a selfish one. It's not what you can put into them . . . it's what you can get out of them. There's a lot like you. You're not alone. but where are your principles?"

Andra knew that Peter was talking the truth. He shrugged. "It's the wey o' the world," he said.

"Aye, your world," Peter said.

"It's hard tae chinge," Andra said quietly. Peter felt he heard remorse in his father's voice.

"Look, dad," he said, "you're not all that bad. You're just stubborn."

"Ach," Andra sighed, "the whole world's goin' balmy. Jean gettin' merried tae . . . an' you . . . how long would it be before ye became a priest, anywey?"

"Oh, about six or eight years . . . depends," Peter replied.

"Well, that's always somethin'," Andra said with some cheer. "Ah could be deid by then."

"What an attitude! Peter said, throwing his hands up in despair. "Think positive, dad. You're not an old man. You could still get into the Masons, the lodge. You just don't know."

Andra brightened up. "Ye think so?" He was surprised at Peter's encouragement. Then, shaking his head, added, "Naw, ye need tae be a bloody contortionist tae get they signals acroass. Ma back jist widnae allow it."

Aye, and you've got to believe in God as well," Peter said.

102

"Whit has God got tae dae wi' it?" Andra said sceptically.

"You've got to believe or you'll never get in either the Masons or the Lodge." Peter said.

Much of what Peter had said was sinking into Andra's deepest thoughts. Annie had never wavered in her faith and Annie was no fool. He had picked up his Daily Record one day and saw a picture of the Queen standing laughing and chatting to an Arab sheik in Buckingham Palace. He wondered about that at the time, but decided that that man was merely inquiring about purchasing the place. He had even seen a minister walking in front of an Orange Walk . . . actually leading it.

Peter was still talking. "And we're all Jock Tamson's bairns," he was saying.

Andra pushed his thoughts to the side.

"Don't talk a loat a rubbish," he said. ·

"We are all made in God's image," Peter replied, ignoring the remark. "You could easily have been born an Eskimo, a Chinese . . . a Jew . . . anything."

"Jist as long as ah wisnae born a catholic," Andra replied. "Ye talk a loat o' tripe at times, Peter. If ah had been born a Chinaman ma faither would definitely hiv been suspicious."

"Do ye not understand what ah'm sayin'?" Peter said.

"Aye, you're sayin' that we are a' born in God's image. How can that be . . . whit colour is HE, then? Do you think that when you get up tae them Pearly Gates ye'll hiv an automatic admission ticket? It'll shake you if ye're met wi' a doorman wi' a big black face an' a turban. Or a wee Chinaman sayin' 'you no getee in here . . . velly solly . . . wrang God'."

"Or even a Mohammedan," Peter laughed.

"They've NAE chance," Andra said shaking his head. "They hivnae a clue."

"They are a very religious race," Peter said, "and ah've no doubt that God is proud of them. They get down on their knees three times a day to pray."

"Aye, ah've seen that oan a TV set. They a' get doon oan their hunkers. Selfish lot, There's wan wee bloke they ignore."

"A wee bloke they ignore?"

"Aye, ah've seen him. Stuck up there on top o' a tower obviously

103

bawlin' for a ladder 'cos he canny get doon. Soon as he starts hollerin' they a' turn their backs an' get doon oan their knees. Could be they're prayin' for a pair o' steps, right enough. '

"Don't be stupid," Peter retorted, "that's a minaret. That man is calling them to prayer."

"Well, they're a' ignoring him anywey," Andra said defiantly.

"Have YOU ever tried praying? It works you know, dad," Peter said.

"Ah do nut believe in it," Andra said, "it disnae work."

"So, you HAVE tried?" Peter said.

"Well, ah did try it at Hampden," Andra said, slightly embarrassed, "but we still got skelped. Ye jist canny compete wi' players fallin' oan their knees an' makin' the sign of the cross."

"I don't believe in that, either," Peter said angrily. "It's provocative and ah think God's got more on his mind than the outcome of a fitba' match."

"Well, y'see it works baith weys," Andra said, glad that he had won one argument."

Peter nodded. "Aye there are faults on both sides . . . but only the minority. Rangers and Celtic supporters do a lot of good charity works just the same as fans in a' the other clubs."

Andra agreed. The two men were silent for a moment. Peter filled two glasses.

"Here," he said to his father, "cheers." They drank. "Now, c'mon," Peter added, "this is Jean's day." Andra nodded, "Aye, it is, isn't it . . ." he said quietly. Annie entered the room pulling on her gloves. She was dressed in a smart two-piece navy blue suit and wore a large, matching felt hat. Andra jumped to his feet. His mouth fell open and he could only stand and stare dumbfounded. It had been a long time since Annie had occasion to dress up. "Aw Annie . . . Annie," Andra said with pride in his voice, "ah hivnae seen ye lookin' as lovely since auld Granny Black's funeral."

"Aye, well it'll be your funeral if ye don't start gettin' ready . . . NOO," Annie bawled but pleased with her husband's compliment.

Turning to Peter, she snapped: "Peter away you in there an' get that hired outfit . . . it's in the big boax."

Peter saluted. "Right," he said and hurried to obey the command. Annie turned to Andra, "Noo YOU . . . get they troosers aff," she ordered.

"It's a bloody long time since ah heard you sayin' that," Andra grinned. "Ye're a catholic right enough . . . wance at Easter or there aboots."

"Ye're nae Robert Redford yersel'," Annie retorted. "When it comes tae the virile stakes . . . you get peched oot jist puttin' yer pyjamas oan."

"Ah've had ma moments," Andra said, slightly hurt.

"Well, ah wish you would hiv telt me aboot them . . . 'cos ah wisnae there," Annie replied. Andra wasn't allowing that remark to pass without retaliation.

"Listen, ah can still turn some wimmen oan," he said stripping to his long johns.

"Andra," Annie said seriously, "the state you come hame in some nights, ye canny even turn the light oan." Andra raised his finger and was about to reply when Peter entered carrying a dress kilt with all the trimmings.

"Here we are," Peter said.

Andra felt the blood rushing to his head. "A kilt! Ah'm no' bloody wearin' THAT," he bawled. Annie ignored his protests. "Peter, get that oan him, she commanded.

There was no point in arguing with Annie, Andra decided. Reluctantly he took the Kilt from Peter and held it up, examining it closely. He frowned and hoped that none of his cronies saw him in this "Rob Roy" outfit. Andra quickly slipped into the kilt . . . on top of his long johns.

"There," he said, doing a twirl, "how dae ah look?" Annie threw a glance towards Heaven. "Get THEM aff," she hollered, pointing to the long underwear . . . Andra shook his head vehemently, "Nut oan yer life," he cried. "these are a' that's between me an' bloody pneumonia."

"If ye don't get them aff, ah'll pull them aff," Annie said advancing on him. Andra quickly rolled up the legs of his longs and tucked them up under the kilt. An inch still showed. "There," he said, "satisfied?"

"Ye don't know how stupit ye look," Annie said in disgust. "Peter, help yer father." Peter, walking towards his bedroom, apologised. "Sorry," he said, "I must get myself ready." Annie hurried to the window and peered out. "The caurs'll be here any minute," she said nervously. "Oh ah wish ah'd went tae an earlier Mass. There widnae hiv been this rush."

"Ah wish ah wis goin' tae Ibrox," Andra muttered. "Well, ah've got somethin', tae tell ye, Andra," Annie said smiling, "Ye're no' goin' tae Ibrox . . . but ye are goin' tae Parkheid soon."

"Whit dae ye mean?" Andra snapped. Annie produced a letter from the sideboard drawer. Waving it under her husband's nose, she said: "Ah got this letter this moarnin'. We've been allocated a multi-storey flat . . . no' a' stanes throw fae Parkheid." She laughed. Andra snatched the letter. "Let me see that," he snarled, quickly glancing through the offending epistle. "Naw . . naw." he said angrily, throwing the letter to the floor and stamping on it repeatedly. "They canny dae that tae me. They're jist tryin' tae break up the stronghold, that's whit it is."

"Aye, an' ah'm gonny ask for the top flair," Annie said enjoying her moment of triumph. "You'll never be nearer Heaven, Andra . . . or should ah say Paradise?" Annie laughed loudly.

"No way am ah goin' there," Andra said angrily. "Aye, ye're goin' a' right," Annie snapped. Andra turned on Annie. 'You've been lightin' they bloody caun'les again, hiven't ye?" he growled.

"Andra, if ah had a penny for every caun'le ah lit for you, ah'd hiv enough for a bungalow.

"He is definitely biased," Andra cried. "Who's biased?" Annie asked. "HIM up there," Andra said, pointing his thumb at the ceiling. "If there IS somebody up there, that is. How is it he listens tae you a' the time? Hiv ah nae say?"

"Hiv ye ever asked Him tae dae ye a favour?" Annie asked. "Ye know whit HE says . . . 'Ask and you wull receive, seek an' you wull find, knock an' it wull be opened unto you'."

"Ah've done a bit o' knockin' in ma time," Andra said, misconstruing Annie's words. "Ye don't get anythin' unless ye ASK," Annie said. "Ye canny expect an answer if ye don't pray."

"Well," Andra said, 'It so happens ah DID pray . . . wance. Ah prayed that ah might get accepted intae the Masons. He either didnae hear me or he IS a Catholic."

"HE only answers yer prayer if it's for yer ain good," Annie said with conviction.

"Aye, maybe ye're right," Andra said, "there was another time ah prayed. It was the night ah was staunin' at the bus stop an' it was pourin' doon. Ah prayed hard that the bus would come. Ah was gettin' soaked."

THE BIGOT

"An' did it?" Annie asked. "Oh aye it came an' knocked me doon. That was the time ah broke ma leg, remember?" Andra grimaced at the thought.

"Aye, well Auld Nick sometimes hears ye as well. He widnae want ye tae be thankful tae HIM in case ye would turn yer coat," Annie said with a smile. "It was a Paki driver," Andra said sourly. "That's got nuthin' tae dae wi' it. It was a wet night, ye said so yersel'." Annie said angrily.

"Anywey," she went on, "Ah canny wait tae see oor new house. Ah'll miss the neighbours though . . . but ah DID hear that Mrs Pringle had been allocated wan o' the flats as well."

"Who the hell's Mrs. Pringle?" Andra had never heard the name mentioned before.

"Oh, jist a wumman ah meet at the shoaps," Annie replied, "so it's nice tae hiv someboady ye know movin' intae a new place wi' ye. She's jist a bit worried her man canny get tae his club. It's a bit awkward, apparently,"

"Big deal," Andra snarled.

"Aye, he's a 'Past Master' or somethin," Annie said, "is that whit ye call it?"

Annie waited to see the sparkle coming into her husband's eye, Andra's eyes lit up. "Is that a fact? Imagine that," he said smiling, "A Past Master', eh? Imagine that . . . Y'know, maybe whoever IS up there does hear two sides tae every story." He shook his head in amazement. He would waste no time in getting acquainted with Mister Pringle.

"Aye, well we'll no' talk aboot it the noo," Annie said, intruding into his euphoric state, "time's gettin' oan. Oh, ah've never been so happy." Annie started to weep. Andra moved to comfort his wife but his embarrassment held him back. "Och . . . er . . . shut yer bawlin'," he paused. "On second thoughts bawl away," he said. Annie continued to weep and Andra threw his caution aside and put his arms around her.

"There there," he said, "hiv yer wee greet." There was a loud rap on the door and Peter hurried in saying "I'll get it."

Andra drew quickly away from his wailing spouse. Peter entered followed by Hughie who wore a frock coat five sizes too big for him. On his head was a squashed-in tiled hat. He flicked a speck of dust from his cream coloured dickey front, which curled up at the bottom.

A shoestring black bow around his neck was the finishing touch to his apparel.

Andra gawked. "Where the hell did ye get that gear?" he bawled. "Ye look like a bloody penguin. Look at him . . . jist look at him," he said, turning to Annie. Hughie eyed Andra up. His long johns had slipped three inches below his kilt. "You've a cheek tae talk aboot me," Hughie said. "YOU look like a Greek sojer, so ye dae."

Andra strutted over and gave Hughie a hefty slap across the shoulder. "You've been tae Paddy's Market, haven't ye? That bloody suit was made for Sidney Greenstreet. Annie hurried to Hughie's rescue. "Never mind, Hughie," she smiled, "ah think ye look lovely!" Annie would not hurt the wee man's feelings, although she did have some misgivings about his appearance. Hughie had tried and that was all that mattered. Hughie was comforted by Annie's concern. He stood back and surveyed the well-dressed wife of his pal with great admiration. "Aw, Annie, so dae you. Ye're jist a picture. Ye look like wan o' they outsized models." Annie smiled and let the side-ways "compliment" pass. She knew what Hughie meant.

"YOU look like a bloody model, tae," Andra snapped, "for gairden gnomes."

A car horn blasted from the street below. Annie rushed to the window and peered out. "That's whit ah came up tae tell ye."

"Oh my God," Annie cried, "no' already. Where's ma hat . . . ma hat . . .?" "It's oan yer heid," Andra said, pacifying his distraught wife.

"So it is," Annie said, after checking. Hughie opened the window and took in the scene below. "The neighbours are a' gatherin'," he cried, ". . . an' there's the baun' jist arrived."

"The baun'? . . . Here . . .? Annie called in panic. "Aye," Hughie said, "ah think they're gonny warm up."

"You're no' even ready," Annie bawled at Andra. Hughie, still surveying the street scene, cried out: "Oh there's big Boozy Bella fae the next close."

"She's probably there for the scramble." Andra sneered, referring to the old tradition where wedding guests throw money from their cars. "Probably tryin' tae get the price o' a boattle o' vino," Andra added. Turning to Annie, he pulled his chest and said, proudly; "Aye, hen, this street's never seen a weddin' like this yin! They're usually takin' the bride straight fae the maternity ward."

"Ah'm no movin' till you get they daft long john's aff." The car horn blasted sending Annie into further panic.

Suddenly the band struck up "It's a Great day for the Irish." Andra stood stunned for a moment, his long john's around his ankles. Then it registered what the song was. He felt the rage start at his toes and rapidly climb until the steam jetted from his ears.

"Dae ye hear whit they're bloody well playin'?" he screamed, kicking away the long johns and leaping on the window sill. "YA STUPIT BLOODY SHOWER," he screamed, hanging halfway out of the window, held on by a panicky Annie, "BOWLY YA BANDY WEE BACHLE . . . AH'LL KILL YE . . ." Annie hauled her husband in. "Get back fae that windae," she screamed. "Ye're gien me a showin' up . . . get in." Andra was fuming. "Ah knew there was something glaiket aboot that daft yin Wullie."

Peter, now in his crisp, dark suit and buttonhole, tugged at his mother's sleeve, "C'mon," he said, "we haven't got much time."

Andra turned to Hughie. "You get doon there this minute, Hughie, an' stoap that racket at wance."

The music stopped and Andra, with a last defiant shake of his fist, came in from the window and flopped on to the couch. Picking up his tartan socks he struggled to get into them.

"Gawd Almighty," he panted, "these soaks are faur too wee. Did ye by any chance git a' this gear fae a shoap that caters for the theatrical profession?" Annie nodded. "So what?" she said.

"Ah thought so," Andra said, struggling to fit them on his feet. "These were made for wan o' the seven dwarfs."

"Probably Dopey," Annie said coldly. Andra ignored the remark and, with a final tug, the socks slipped on. Andra sighed after his struggle and picked up the dark, leather shoes, examining them closely. "Whit kind o' bloody shoes are these?" he said with a grimace.

"Pigskin," Annie replied.

"Pigskin?" Andra said sullenly. "That's the nearest we'll get tae ham at this weddin."

The music suddenly started up again in the street. Andra's ears pricked up and a broad smile flitted across his face. The sound of The Sash My Father Wore filled the street. The song of the Orange Lodge marches filled his heart to bursting and Andra jumped for joy.

Leaping from the couch he jumped on to the window sill with one bound, pulling the window down from the top, he hung over. "Come oan ya beauty," he cried, half out of the window. His kilt swung in time to the rousing music."Oh, whit a showin' up, Annie groaned, "C'mon Peter. Let's get oot o' here."

Annie and Peter hurried from the house as an ecstatic Andra bellowed, "Gie it laldy, Wullie," He jumped down from the sill and, swinging his sporran, marched up and down the room in time to the music. "Come oan ra boys," he bawled. The music got louder and Andra more frenzied. Suddenly the tempo changed as Wullie and his boys swung into Bei Mir Bist Du Shon, a rousing Jewish song. Andra stopped in mid stride and hopped on to the window sill. Leaning over, he bawled angrily at Wullie; 'Whit the hell's THAT ye're playin'?"

"A good Jewish song," Wullie hollered.

"Well, chuck it this minute ye eejit. THIS is a non-secterian weddin' . . . play Ra Sash again."

Wullie shrugged and the band struck up The Sash. "Good oan ye," Andra cried happily, joining in with the lyrics for the benefit of the folk below

Andra came down from the window, poured himself another drink and flopped on to the couch. Despite his objections to the wedding, he was proud of the turnout downstairs. He would show them! The street had not changed much since his boyhood. Auld Maggie from up the pend looked as old now as she did all those years ago: She used to come out of her house, still clutching her bottle of "Red Biddy" and chase the boys, cursing them for disturbing her peace. Andra smiled. They were scamps, all of them. Finbar Cassidy was the leader of the gang. What a boy he was! 'Didn't Finbar go to the Sacred Heart School? And didn't they go to Parkhead now and then to see Celtic play?' Wee Manny Jacobwitz used to go with them. If they did not go to Parkhead, they went to the Arcadia Cinema on Saturday afternoons . . . Buck Jones, Gene Autrey and their blazing guns. The boys would hurry home after the pictures, skelping their backside all the way . . . urging their "horses" to go faster and faster. Manny's mum, the largest lady in the street, made patchwork quilts and sold them cheaply to the neighbours. They were beautiful and reminded Andra of magic carpets. Funny, he never thought of Manny as a Jew. They were all just boys . . . pals. And there was Archie McLaughlin whose father wore the orange sash every July the twelfth. He looked magnificent as took his place in the annual Orange Walk. Finbar, Manny and Andra were always there to cheer him on. Andra smiled as he remembered.

It was only as your grew older that prejudice entered your life. Andra was suddenly deep in thought.

He did not hear Jean enter the room. "DAD," she called loudly . . ."DAD." Andra turned. He stared at his daughter . . . beautiful in her gleaming white wedding dress. He had never seen Jean look so lovely. He suddenly felt embarrassed. His eyes were moist and he was confused for a moment. He drew the back of his hand across his eyes. "Bloody grit," he mumbled.

"Well," Jean said, doing a sedate twirl, "what do you think?" Andra took Jean by the hands and stood back at arms length. She was perfect in every way. "Ma Jean," he said softly, "ma bonnie Jean . . . ye're . . . ye're . . ." he searched for words, "like a film star," he said finally. Jean smiled. The street music struck up The Anniversary Waltz and Jean pulled her father towards her. "Let's have a wee dance before we go." Andra shuffled his feet," Ach, ah hivnae danced since ma Barraland days," he said coyly.

"You'll manage," Jean said, and they waltzed around the floor. "Here, there's a bit of the Fred Astaire in you," Jean laughed, "a bit of a dark horse, eh? Are you sure you haven't been takin' lessons?"

"Ach, away wi ye!" he said blushing, "It's like goin' a bike, ye never forget." As they danced around the floor, nostalgia once more swept over him. Annie was in his arms. They were in Barraland and Billy Macgregor's band was playing the tune. Annie was laughing as the always did when they were out together. There weren't many laughs now. Andra came back to reality. He felt uncomfortable. This music was too doleful.

"We'd better watch oor time," he said, breaking off the dance.

'You're right, dad," Jean agreed. Andra put on the finishing touches to his attire and looked at himself with satisfaction in the wall mirror. He had acquired a flower for his buttonhole at the botanical section of the peoples' Palace, at Glasgow Green. "Hiv ye got a pin, Jean?" he asked, holding up his flower. Jean gaped. "What's that, dad?"

"Yer mither told me tae get a flooer," he said. Jean took the flower from him. "NOT an orange lily, dad,"she said shaking her head. She plucked a carnation from her bouquet and fastened it to her father's lapel. "There," she said, standing back admiringly, "you look very handsome, dad."

Andra grinned. "Ah'm gonny miss ye, Jean. It'll be funny no' hivin' a lassie aroon' the hoose."

"Well, Maureen's looking for good digs," Jean said, "why don't you let her have my room?"

"She's a Buddhist!" Andra exclaimed.

"That shouldn't matter. She would pay her way."

"Mair rupees widnae go amiss," Andra joked.

They laughed. Maureen entered the room and gave a twirl.

"Well," she said.

Jean kissed her lightly on the cheek. "You're lovely," she said.

Andra nodded in agreement. "Aye, ye're a wee stoater," he said.

The street music had stopped and Andra only just noticed. He leaped on to the window sill and bawled down at Wullie. "Whit's the gemme there? Are youse oan strike or somethin'?" The band struck up with the Sash once more and Andra could not contain himself. He roared with delight and swayed with the music . . . faster and faster as the tempo quickened. He did not see the soap. His foot came down heavily on it. Up in the air Andra went with a shriek and . . . out of the window he went, plummeting to the street below.

CHAPTER SIX

HOSPITAL

Andra's eyes flickered. The smell of antiseptic wafted across his nostrils. He could feel his hand being squeezed tenderly and a soft voice saying, "Come along now, Mr Thomson, that's the boy." Slowly he opened his eyes. A face, blurred at first, sharpened into focus. The young, pretty nurse smiled. "That's it, come on now."

Andra tried to raise himself but fell back on to the pillow, gently pushed. "Now, now you must lie still," the nurse said.

"Where am ah?" he muttered.

"You're in the Royal Infirmary," the nurse said, feeling his pulse. "I'll just fetch the doctor." Andra heard her footsteps fade in the distance. He lay still for a moment, getting his bearings. He breathed deeply. The strong clinical smell made him cough. Easing himself up on one elbow, he looked around the ward. There were just three beds in the small ward. To his right he could see a man, his leg up in traction with an arm raised stiffly above his head in plaster. The third bed was empty.

"How are ye feelin', Andra?" Hughie's voice came from somewhere in the bandaged face.

"Is that you, Hughie?" Andra said with surprise.

"It's me a' right," the voice replied.

"Ah didnae recognise ye without yer bunnet," Andra said. "Whit happened tae ye?"

"You bloody fell right oan tap o' me," Hughie grumbled. "ye squashed ma hat."

"Aw, Hughie, ah'm helluva sorry. A' ah remember was leanin' ower the windae an' then nuthin'" Andra's contrition was genuine. "Ye look like ye've had a good dunt," he added.

"Ye don't look so hot yersel'," Hughie replied. "Feel yer heid,"

Andra's hands went up to his head. It was swathed in bandages. "Oh, geez," he moaned, "ah hope there's nae permanent damage! Never tae wear ma blue an' white titfer would be mair than ah could bear."

"Aye, ye look daft right enough," Hughie stated.

"AH, look daft? YOU look like you're doin' the bloody goose-step an' gein' the Heil Hitler salute," Andra snapped. "If yer other airm had a stookie oan it, wi' a coat of paint and a fishin' rod, you could get a joab as a gairden gnome."

Andra's sarcasm fell on deaf ears.

"Never mind," Hughie said, "we're in the right place. They can dae wonders in here. See that empty bed ower there? Well, when you were oot cold, the man that was in that bed was allowed hame after an amazin' operation."

"Whit was up wi' him?" Andra asked with interest.

"He had an erse transplant," Hughie said with quiet admiration.

Andra was astonished at this wonder of modern surgery. "Geez, that's amazin' right enough," he uttered "Are ye sure?"

"Definitely," Hughie said, "he told me hisel'. He got locked in the freezer in the butcher's where he worked. It was 'oors before they got tae him an' when they pulled him oot his erse fell aff. They said it was frostbite."

"Away, ya eejit," Andra said, "it would be his EARS that fell aff. They could replace them a' right . . . a dod o' plasticine or somethin'."

"Or even wax," Hughie added.

"Naw, they widnae use wax," Andra said, "melts too easy. Could ye imagine him staunin' in the pub under the heater bletherin' away tae some big blonde, given her the patter an' suddenly his ears begin tae melt?"

The nurse with the soft voice entered and immediately began to fluff Andra's pillow's and make him more comfortable.

"The doctor will be in shortly, Mr Thomson," she said, "and your family's been waiting. I'll send them in." Nurse Soft Voice departed as quickly as she had arrived. Seconds later the door opened. Andra fell back on his pillow and groaned quietly.

Annie entered followed by Peter, Jean and Clarence. "There, there," Annie said, sitting at the bedside and squeezing Andra's hand with tenderness. "How are ye feelin'?"

"Aw, ah'm dyin'," Andra moaned. Jean kissed her father softly on the cheek. "You'll be all right," she said. "You had a lucky escape!" Peter exclaimed. Clarence nodded. They offered their commiserations to Hughie who mumbled his thanks.

"Did ye .. er . . . bring a wee hauf boattle," Andra asked timidly. Annie sat bolt upright. Andra was playing up. He still had a clear eye and was looking for sympathy.

THE BIGOT

"Ye can forget hauf boattles, quarter boattles an' even miniatures for a while," she growled. "Jist be thankful ye're a' right."

"Ye call THIS a'right?" Andra said pointing to his head. "How long hiv ah been unconscious?"

"Ever since ah've known ye," Annie snapped.

"Whit aboot the weddin'?"

"We postponed it, dad," Jean said with a sniff. "Yes," Clarence nodded, "We couldn't have the wedding without you being there."

Andra's chest puffed out. "Ye . . . er . . . were thinkin' o' me?" he said with a slight cough, concealing his pride.

"Of course," Clarence said. "We couldn't have Jean walking down the aisle by herself, could we?"

Andra felt a lump in his throat. He held back. "Aye, well . . . er . . . it'll no' be long before ah'm oan ma feet," he said.

"Ye loast a lot o' blood, Andra," Annie said. "When the doactors tested it for transfusion purposes they didnae know whether tae put it in the clinical cabinet or the drinks cabinet." They laughed, Andra joining in, with titters from Hughie.

"Did YOU know that you've a very special blood group — AB Negative — ?" Annie asked. "An' they had tae make an appeal for donors?"

"Well, ah always knew that ah was somethin' special," Andra laughed.

"Special Brew, ye mean," Annie quipped. "Ah take it that they got the donors a'right?" Andra said, holding his head.

"Aye, two o' the wedding guests who gie blood regularly knew right away that their blood was compatible an' volunteered immediately."

"That was good o' them," Andra said. "Who was it, then?"

"The Rabbi an' Father McGinty," Annie said, hiding a smile. Andra was silent for a moment. This was contamination:

"WHIT?" he bellowed . . . "Ah'm lyin' here lookin' like a bloody sikh wi' Jewish an' Catholic blood pulsin' through ma veins?"

Hughie, behind his bandages, bounced uncontrollably on the bed laughing uproarously as far as his injuries would allow.

"No' only THAT," Annie added, "yer Rangers pals rallied roon as well . . . along wi' some o' the CELTIC supporters fae doon the road." She waited for the explosion. It did not come. Andra was quiet. He had not bargained on this. Jean broke the silence.

115

"We'll go into the corridor for a coffee from the machine and leave you two alone for a while." she said. They slipped quietly away. Annie squeezed her husband's hand. "Y'see, Andra," she said softly, "people ARE good deep doon. A' that blood ye got was the same colour. Even Mr Ali who's got the wee newsagents shoap came forward tae help." Andra found it difficult to find the right words.

"Aye, well . . . er . . . it jist shows ye, dint it?" he said finally.

"You jist get well soon," Annie said tenderly, "an' the weddin' will go ahead . . . that's if ye've nae objections?"

"ME OBJECTIONS?" Andra held Annie's hand tightly. "Ye've put up wi' a loat, hen, hivent ye?"

"Yer ma man, Andra."

"Aye, ah am, aren't ah? Ah'll turn ower a new leaf, Annie."

"Jist be a bit mair tolerant, Andra," Annie whispered. "We're a' in this wee world together."

"Aye," Andra said, deep in thought, then bringing his head up quickly, added — "But ah'm only sorry ah never got intae the Masons or the Ludge. It wisnae tae be."

"Naebody's askin' ye tae stoap tryin', Andra," Annie replied. "They baith dae good charity work jist like the Knights O' Saint Columba an' the Jewish charities an' the Pakistanis an' Indians an' everbody else."

"Naw," Andra said decidedly, "Ah'm finished noo, away oot there an' tell Peter an' Clarence that ah want tae see them."

"Whit for?" Annie asked, furrowing her brow.

"Jist go oot an' send them in," Andra commanded. Annie left the room with a backward, worried glance. Andra turned to Hughie. "Noo, you've been listenin' tae a' this Hughie. keep yer mooth shut."

"Ah'm yer pal, Andra," Hughie muttered. "Ah know, Hughie," Andra replied to his faithful friend. Then, talking more to himself than his crony, bit his lip in disbelief. "Imagine they Celtic Supporters . . . imagine that!"

Peter and Clarence entered together. "Sit doon," Andra said, indicating the chairs. "Clarence," he began quietly, "Ah hope ye'll forgive me, son. You an' ma Jean will be very happy an' ah'm jist sorry that ah made things difficult for ye."

"Clarence took Andra's outstretched hand. "Forget it," he said.

"An', Peter," Andra said, turning to his son, "ye can come intae McDougall's any time ye like. In fact we can even go ower tae

116

Rafferty's pub noo an' again . . .noo that ah've got some Celtic blood in me."

They laughed together. Their laughter was interrupted by the doctor's entrance. Peter and Clarence arose. "We'll get away, dad, an' leave you to it," Peter said. Andra nodded. When the boys got to the door, Andra called. "An' Clarence," he said, 'ye can bring the weans up anytime," Peter and Clarence laughed and left the room. Andra lay back on his pillow.

"Well, Mr Thomson," the doctor said smiling, "and how are we today?"

"No bad," Andra replied and gave a groan.

"You'll be on your feet in no time," the doctor said. "I'm Doctor Mason, by the way."

"MASON?" was this a signal, Andra wondered?

"Tell me, doactor," he said, "has your granny got a wart on her bum?"

"EH?", the doctor answered, his mouth falling open.

Andra grinned.